"Oh, Chelsey," Mitch murmured as he caressed her shoulders. "I want you so much. So very much."

Her name, Mitch's voice . . . they were real. They suddenly brought back the room, the sofa, the dog sleeping on the floor. Oh, no, Chelsey thought, swallowing the sob in her throat, the clock had chimed midnight and Cinderella was home.

"Mitch, no," she whispered. "I'm sorry, I should never have let you . . . it wasn't fair. I led you to believe I was willing to . . . I'm sorry."

"What are you saying, Chelsey?"

"I told you I flunked liberation, Mitch," she said, blinking back her tears. "I'm very glad I met you, though, and—"

"Wait a minute, Chelsey, are you dusting me off?"

"Well, why would you hang around if—"

"Thanks a lot!" he yelled. "Is that what you think of me, that I won't be interested if you don't go to bed with me? What am I, a sex maniac? Maybe I was acting like one, but . . . I won't be put off that easily, Chelsey. You make me smile and laugh, and you drive me nuts, and you're wonderful. I looked at a sunset to-night because of you. I want to see you and be with you and—"

"Why are you hollering at me?" Chelsey asked.

"I'm not! Well, yes, I am. Chelsey, we'll take it slow and easy, I promise. Now, I'm going home and you're going to bed. Alone. But you haven't seen the last of me, Chelsey Star . . ."

WHAT ARE *LOVESWEPT* ROMANCES?

They are stories of true romance and touching emotion. We believe those two very important ingredients are constants in our highly sensual and very believable stories in the *LOVESWEPT* line. Our goal is to give you, the reader, stories of consistently high quality that may sometimes make you laugh, sometimes make you cry, but are always fresh and creative and contain many delightful surprises within their pages.

Most romance fans read an enormous number of books. Those they truly love, they keep. Others may be traded with friends and soon forgotten. We hope that each *LOVESWEPT* romance will be a treasure—a "keeper." We will always try to publish

LOVE STORIES YOU'LL NEVER FORGET
BY AUTHORS YOU'LL ALWAYS REMEMBER

The Editors

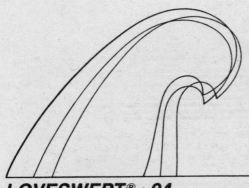

LOVESWEPT® • *94*

Joan Elliott Pickart
Waiting for
Prince Charming

BANTAM BOOKS
TORONTO • NEW YORK • LONDON • SYDNEY • AUCKLAND

WAITING FOR PRINCE CHARMING

A Bantam Book / May 1985

*LOVESWEPT® and the wave device are registered
trademarks of Bantam Books, Inc. Registered in U.S. Patent
and Trademark Office and elsewhere.*

ISBN 0-553-21706-2

Published simultaneously in the United States and Canada

---

*Bantam Books are published by Bantam Books, Inc. Its
trademark, consisting of the words "Bantam Books" and
the portrayal of a rooster, is Registered in U.S. Patent and
Trademark Office and in other countries. Marca Registrada.
Bantam Books, Inc., 666 Fifth Avenue, New York, New
York 10103.*

PRINTED IN THE UNITED STATES OF AMERICA

O   0 9 8 7 6 5 4 3 2 1

For my editor, Elizabeth Barrett,
and her magical telephone

One

Chelsey Star blew a large pink bubble with the wad of gum in her mouth, tugged her baseball cap firmly into place, and strode to the plate.

"Okay," she yelled, "heads up out there. I want some sharp fielding. Keep your eye on the ball!"

The squad of ten- and eleven-year-old girls in every shape and size imaginable waved cheerfully. Chelsey tapped her bat on the plate, then swung it up over her shoulder.

"Throw it right across here, Patsy," Chelsey said, "so I can hit it out to them."

"Strike one!" the catcher yelled a moment later.

"Yeah, well, I missed," Chelsey mumbled.

"You can say that again," the chubby catcher said.

"I'm the coach, not Reggie Jackson," Chelsey said. "I'll get the next one."

"Strike two!" the little girl hollered as the bat again connected with nothing.

"Slow it down a little, Patsy," Chelsey said. "We're supposed to be having fielding practice here, and it would help if I got the ball out there."

"Here it comes!" Patsy yelled.

Crack!

Chelsey hit the ball with such force that the bat stung her hands and she dropped it as though it were a hot potato. With wide eyes she watched the missile go sailing over the heads of the astonished fielders and disappear beyond the chain-link fence surrounding the field.

"Hey, how about that?" Chelsey said. "Pretty good, huh?"

"Terrific," the catcher said. "We just lost our ball."

"Oh, heavens." Chelsey took off at a run. "Come on!"

The team headed for the fence, accompanied by an enormous brindle-colored Great Dane, barking at a high volume, who loped along in the midst of the group. The throng came to a halt when they reached the gate and the huge dog tumbled over his own feet, landing in a heap beside Chelsey.

"Zork, get up," Chelsey said. "See? You've messed up your glasses."

The animal struggled to his feet and stood patiently while Chelsey adjusted the elastic straps over his ears that held a pair of sunglasses securely in front of his eyes.

"There," she said. "Now, let's find the—"

"Oh, no!" someone shrieked. "Look at that!"

All heads turned and a gasp escaped from Chelsey's lips. The missing ball had been found. It was resting on the hood of a royal blue sports car that boasted a very thoroughly cracked windshield.

"It's a Ferrari," Patsy shrieked. "They cost a million dollars! The owner will put a contract out on our lives! We're dead meat!"

"Patsy, hush," Chelsey said. "Are you sure that's a Ferrari? Maybe it's just a fancy Chevy."

"No way," the girl said. "I'm too young to die! I wanna go home!"

"Maybe that's a good idea," Chelsey said. "You guys take off and I'll wait for the owner of the car and explain what happened. Remember, be here at ten sharp tomorrow morning for the game. It's the last one of the season and we're going to win!"

"Why break a perfect record?" a small voice muttered.

"Bad attitude, Becky," Chelsey said. "Just because we've lost every one so far doesn't mean we can't finish up in a blaze of glory. Off you go, gang. Make sure your T-shirts are clean and be ready to play ball!"

"I'm tellin' ya, we're dead meat," Patsy said. "I betcha the owner of that Ferrari is in the Mafia. A hitman! A gangster!"

"I'm ignoring you, Patsy," Chelsey said. "Wait here a minute while I get the ball."

Chelsey slipped through an opening in the fence with Zork close on her heels and cringed as she approached the sleek automobile. She carefully plucked the ball off the hood and tossed it over to the girls.

"Tomorrow morning, ten sharp," she said.

A round of good-byes was exchanged as the group dispersed, then Chelsey planted her hands on her slim hips and frowned at the injured vehicle.

The sun was dancing off the gleaming blue finish and the shiny wire hubcaps, and the cracked windshield boasted several inches of a smoky-colored tint. It was obvious that no expense had been spared on this car. Chelsey moaned.

"We've got trouble, Zork," she said to the dog, who wagged his tail happily. "Do you really think that's a Ferrari?"

With a sigh, Chelsey lowered her five-foot-four-inch frame to the ground and rested her back against the fence, stretching her tanned legs out in front of her. Zork plopped down next to her and she absently straightened the sunglasses over his eyes.

She had no choice but to wait for the owner of the car. She'd ridden over to the practice field on her bike and had no way of leaving a note. She could only hope the hitman—no, he was not!—wasn't off on an all-day excursion somewhere. The sun was climbing higher in the sky and despite the slight breeze, the end of August day was becoming increasingly hot. In typical San Diego fashion it was also humid. Chelsey blew a breath of air up over her face, then produced another large pink bubble.

A few minutes later she looked up expectantly as two joggers approached along the running path, but when they thudded on past, she settled back against the fence.

"Some buddy you are," she said to Zork, who had rested his head on Chelsey's leg and fallen asleep.

After a half-hour, Chelsey was toying with the idea of seeing if the car was unlocked so she could obtain the owner's name from the registration and contact him later. She was cooking, and could feel the perspiration running down between her full breasts.

Out of the corner of her eye she saw another jogger approaching and made up her mind that if this wasn't the person she was waiting for, she was resorting to plan B. The man slowed his pace and stopped about twenty feet from where she was sitting. Her gaze flickered over his well-proportioned body clad in running shorts and a sweat-stained T-shirt. He was tall, probably over six feet, and had the tightly muscled physique of an athlete. Wide shoulders were set across a broad expanse of chest that tapered to a trim waist and narrow hips. His tousled mass of thick blond hair suddenly disappeared as the man pulled the shirt over his head and away, using it to mop his face and chest.

Chelsey blinked once slowly, her gaze riveted on him. He was incredible. He looked as though he'd stepped off a billboard or out of a fashion magazine. A curly mass of tawny hair covered his chest and narrowed into the waistband of his shorts. As he walked slowly toward her, Chelsey pushed herself to her feet, startling Zork awake and causing the dog to scramble up. She swallowed heavily, not sure why her heart was suddenly racing. Either she was afraid she was about to face the owner of the Ferrari, or this epitome of virility was really shaking her up.

It hardly seemed fair that a man who had been dished

out a body like that should get such a gorgeous face thrown in for good measure. Deeply tanned, his features were rugged and even, with high cheekbones, a straight nose, and square chin. Blond eyebrows were raised slightly when he saw Chelsey and his blue eyes did a quick but thorough scrutiny of her attractive figure. She instantly wondered if her white shorts were too short, her green T-shirt too tight. His gaze came to rest on Zork, and the man took a step backward.

"Good Lord," he said in a rich, deep voice, "what is that? A horse?"

"It's a Great Dane," Chelsey said.

"Wearing sunglasses? I've been out in the heat too long!"

"Excuse me, but is this your car?"

"Yeah, it's a beauty, isn't it? I just got it and—oh, my God!" the man bellowed. "What in the hell happened here? Would you look at my windshield?"

"Please don't get excited," Chelsey said, raising her hands in a peace-seeking gesture. "I can explain. You see—"

"Your horse sat on it, right?" he yelled.

"Zork is a dog!"

"Who thinks he's a movie star so he wears shades? I can't believe this! What did you clobber my car with?"

"A baseball."

"So who are you, Reggie Jackson?"

"No. In fact, I had just said that was who I wasn't when I hit the home run."

"Huh?"

"Look—um—I'm really sorry about this and—"

"Sorry! Do you know what this is going to cost?"

"Don't you have insurance?" she asked hopefully.

"It goes into effect at midnight tonight. I just bought this car. See the sticker in the back window?"

"Oh, dear. I guess I'll have to pay for it, then."

"You bet your life, toots."

"Well, you don't have to be rude! I've been sitting here waiting for you, hotshot. I could have just taken off, you know."

"Oh, I would have found you. I'm sure there were witnesses and you'd be easy to spot. How many bald women are there in San Diego who roam around with a horse that wears sunglasses?"

"Bald? Who's bald?"

"Is there hair under that hat?"

"There certainly is," Chelsey snapped, whipping the cap off her head. A cascade of thick, wavy auburn-colored hair tumbled to her shoulders and she looked up at the man defiantly. "Satisfied?"

"Very," he said quietly, reaching out and running the fingers of one large hand through the tresses. "It's lovely."

Again Chelsey's heart did a funny little dance. She took a quick breath as the man's thumb trailed across her cheek as he withdrew his hand. He stared down at her from his lofty height, and their eyes met and held for a long moment. Chelsey had to remind herself to breathe.

The sun was glistening over the moist, curly hair on the man's chest and across the muscles of his shoulders and upper arms. The thumb that had caressed her cheek was work-roughened and hard, but had possessed a gentleness as it moved across her soft skin. Only one word came to Chelsey's mind. Wow!

"Yes! Well!" she said, pulling herself out of her semitrance. "About the car."

"I have to ask," the man said, shaking his head. "I really do. Why does that animal have on sunglasses?"

"He has sensitive eyes, a genetic disorder."

"Oh."

"The owner was going to put him to sleep, but I took him. He was only a puppy and he's turned into a beautiful dog, don't you think?"

"He's awfully big. Does he bite?"

"Not so far."

"That's reassuring." He frowned. "Okay, Mickey Mantle, let's discuss my windshield. It's going to cost a bundle."

"How much?"

"I don't know, I'll have to take it into the shop. Damn, a brand-new car!"

"It's a Chevy, right?"

"Are you nuts? That's a Ferrari, lady."

"I was afraid of that," Chelsey mumbled.

"Oh, man," he said, dropping his chin to his chest and planting his hands on his hips.

Chelsey stared up at him with the irrational thought that she'd like to cradle him in her arms and tell him everything would be all right. They'd get his new toy fixed and he shouldn't be so upset. She tilted her head slightly and studied him further. He was beautiful, absolutely beautiful. It was as though he had been sculpted out of stone with precision workmanship and then bronzed to perfection. He was masculinity personified in a pair of jogging shorts, and Chelsey felt a startling flutter within her. The man even smelled male! The heady aroma of his perspiration reached her nostrils and she was suddenly aware there were several different shades of blond in his hair. She bet his eyes sparkled when he smiled, which he wasn't about to do because she had creamed his precious, dumb flash-and-dash car.

"Are you going to pass out or something?" she asked.

"I'm thinking it over. I wish you were a man so I could pop you in the chops."

"Thanks a bunch! I didn't do it on purpose, you know! And I did wait here like a good citizen."

"Hooray for you," he growled, striding to the car and yanking open the door. He tossed the T-shirt inside and reached for another one that was on the seat.

What a shame, Chelsey thought as he pulled on the yellow shirt. He was covering up that lovely scenery. Not that there was anything wrong with the way the shirt molded itself to his broad chest and clung to the flat plane of his stomach. Nothing wrong at all! The man was so darn gorgeous it was ridiculous!

He turned and plunked himself sideways onto the bucket seat, his long, muscular legs stretching out into the parking lot. Chelsey stood perfectly still, wondering what was going to happen next, and jumped in alarm when the man bellowed, "Come over here, Pete Rose!"

"Would you quit hollering!" she yelled, stomping around the open door and standing in front of him. Zork immediately joined her.

"Well, I'm upset, damm it! I go for a nice run and come back to this! What do you expect? That I'd kiss you out of gratitude for playing demolition derby?"

"I wouldn't want you to kiss me for any reason!"

"Oh?" His voice was suddenly low and quiet. "Would you care to discuss that in more depth?"

Chelsey opened her mouth to retort, then closed it immediately as she realized she didn't know what to say. She became acutely aware that the man's leg was pressing against hers and she could feel the heat emanating from that muscular limb. He was looking at her steadily, his blue eyes seeming to lock onto her mahogany brown ones and hold her immobile. A silence that was probably only seconds long stretched into infinity, and Chelsey felt a strange warmth start somewhere within her and travel like tingling fingers throughout her body.

"What's your name?" the man asked finally, his eyes not leaving hers.

"Chelsey Star," she said softly.

"Hello, Chelsey Star. I'm Mitch Brannon."

Zork chose that moment to wag his tail vigorously, whopping Chelsey on the bottom and snapping her out of the spell she had fallen under. Mitch, too, seemed to come back to earth and reached above the visor for paper and a pen.

"Address? Phone?" he said, his voice crisp and businesslike.

Chelsey rattled off the information after drawing a steadying breath. What had happened? Mitch Brannon had looked at her and she had been rendered speechless, unable to move. He had a magnetism that upset her equilibrium and she did not care for it. No, not one little bit!

"Age?" he said.

"Twenty-four."

"Married?"

"No. Hey, what has my age and marital status got to do with anything?"

"Nothing. Just instinct, I guess. I see a pretty woman and I want to know all her vital statistics."

"So what's next? My measurements?"

"Nope, I've got those already," he said, his gaze roaming lazily over her figure.

"You're nervy, do you know that? Just send me a bill for your crummy windshield."

"And you'll pay for it?"

"Yes! Well, not all at once. It will have to be in installments."

"Wonderful." He frowned. "Damn, that dog makes me nervous. With those sunglasses on I can't see where he's looking. Maybe he's deciding I'd make a tasty lunch."

Chelsey shrugged. "Could be."

"Tell him to go away."

"No!"

"He bites me and I'll sue the panties off you, Chelsey Star!"

"I'll take my chances, Mitch Brannon!"

"Brother! So tell me, slugger, what happened to the rest of your team? They cop out when you got in trouble here?"

"No, I sent them home. I hit the ball and it's my responsibility."

"Nice guys. Left you holding the bag."

"They're just little girls, for Pete's sake."

"You play ball with kids? What happened? Did the major leagues drop your contract?"

"I'm their coach!"

"You're a baseball coach? You?" He suddenly burst into laughter.

The sound was mellow, a rich timbre that seemed to rumble up from the depth of Mitch's chest and dance across the air. The smile that accompanied it showed straight white teeth and made him appear younger than his approximately thirty-five years. His features took on almost boyish qualities and he seemed less threatening and angry. Chelsey smiled in return.

"Yes, I'm the coach," she said, "of the Orange Crushers."

"Is your team any good?"

"We have a lot of spirit."

"Meaning they're lousy."

"Well, we didn't win any, but tomorrow is the last game and I have high hopes that we'll go out with a victory."

"Is that what you do for a living? Coach losing Little League teams?" Mitch asked.

"Of course not! I took it on as an extra job for the summer."

"What do you do to pay the rent?"

"I'm a computer systems analyst."

"Whew! The pretty lady has brains. That's good to know. I hate bubbleheads."

"Look, Mitch, it's getting hot out here. Let's agree on a way for me to pay for the damage to your car and be done with it."

"A way to pay? Now this could get interesting." He chuckled, the throaty sound causing a slight shiver to tingle down Chelsey's spine.

This would never do, she thought. Mitch was rattling her, setting her off balance with his handsome good looks, incredible body, and veiled innuendos. She had to get a grip on herself.

"I meant," she said firmly, "how much money I'd give you every month! How does ten dollars sound?"

"Ten! Are you crazy? I'll be dead and buried before you finish it off!"

"You don't even know how much it's going to cost!"

"Well, it will be plenty, that's for sure."

"Serves you right for getting such a showboat car."

"What in the hell is the matter with it?" he roared.

"Nothing, I suppose. I imagine a lot of playboys drive those."

"Who said I was a playboy? That's a rotten thing to say, Chelsey!"

"Well, excuse me! But what do you expect me to think? Sleek machine, nonstop body, typical California tan. It all adds up to playboy!"

"You like my body?" he asked, grinning at her.

"Oh, forget it! Good-bye!" She turned to walk away.

"Hold it!" Mitch said, grabbing her arm. "We're not finished here."

"Get your hand off me or I'll tell Zork to have you for a snack!"

"Lord." He quickly released her and eyed the dog warily. "Tell him you think I'm terrific. Is he looking at me? I really hate those sunglasses."

"Will you accept ten dollars a month or not?" Chelsey asked, planting her hands on her hips.

"We'll discuss it when I get the bill."

"Fine. Good day, Mr. Brannon."

"Wait! I might as well give you a ride home. It's really warming up out here."

"No, thank you. I have my bike right over— Oh damn, damn," Chelsey shrieked.

"What's wrong?" Mitch yelled, jerking up from the seat so quickly that he bumped his head on the door-jamb. "Ow! Dammit! That hurt! I swear, woman, you are dangerous to have around!"

"Did you break the skin?" she asked anxiously, staring up at him as he towered above her. "Bend over and let me see."

Mitch did as instructed and Chelsey tentatively placed her fingertips on his head. His hair was thick, but felt silky to her touch and slightly moist from perspiration. The pungent male aroma once more assaulted her senses as she gently explored the top of Mitch's nicely shaped head. The hair definitely had several shades, ranging from almost white-blond where the sun had bleached it to light brown below the surface. Chelsey idly lifted the thick crop, letting it tumble back into place as it slid through her fingers.

It was such nice, nice hair, she thought dreamily. Just really . . . nice.

"Well?" Mitch said.

"Huh? Oh, you just have a little bump." She dropped her hands and took a step backward.

"What in the hell were you screaming about?"

"Me? Oh! Oh, my bike! It's gone! My wonderful bike has been ripped off!"

"Are you sure? Where was it?"

"Over there across the field by that bench. This is all your fault, Mitch Brannon."

"Mine? I didn't steal your crummy bike!"

"If I hadn't been sitting over here waiting for you this never would have happened. I've had that bike since I was twelve years old! It was beat-up and ugly and I loved it! Oh, damn," she said as tears sprang to her eyes.

"Hey, take it easy," he said gently, wrapping his arms around her and pulling her to his chest. "Don't cry."

Goodness, he felt good, Chelsey thought wildly. That chest was rock-hard and his arms were strong, giving her an instant feeling of well-being. Maybe she'd stay right there for an hour or two and simply enjoy. She could feel Mitch's heart beating in a steady rhythm while hers was dancing a jig. How could a sweaty man smell so good? All of that did not, however, erase the fact that her bike had disappeared off the face of the earth!

"Oh, this is awful," she said, extracting herself rather reluctantly from Mitch's embrace.

"Let's go over there and look around," he said. "Maybe someone just moved it to give you a hard time. I mean, if it's that old, who would want it?"

"It's a classic!"

"Okay, don't get hysterical." He slammed the car door shut. "I don't suppose your horse would wait here?"

"Of course not."

"Didn't think so."

A thorough search of the far side of the field turned up nothing and Chelsey sank onto the bench, resting her elbows on her knees and cupping her chin in her hands. Mitch sat down next to her and patted her on the back.

"Are you going to cry some more?" he asked quietly.

"No, it wouldn't help. I guess you think I'm nuts to care so much about an old, beat-up thing, but it was the last present my father gave me before he died. I was very sentimentally attached to it."

"I'm sorry, Chelsey."

"Well, thanks for helping me look for it. I hope whoever took it falls off and breaks his leg."

"Sounds fair. Come on, I'll give you a ride home."

"Zork won't fit in your swanky car."

"Can't he run alongside?"

"No!"

"Well, I just can't leave you here looking—looking sad, for Pete's sake," he said, raking his hand through his hair.

"I'll walk. It's only a couple of miles. Listen, let me know about the windshield."

"Yeah." Mitch got to his feet. "I'll be in touch. Are you sure you're all right?"

"Yes, I'm fine."

"Well, see ya, Chelsey."

" 'Bye, Mitch. I really am sorry about your car. That was the first home run I ever hit in my life."

Mitch started off across the field, only to stop about halfway over and glance back at Chelsey. She hadn't moved from her dejected pose on the bench. With a defeated sigh, he threw up his hands and sprinted back to her.

"Sit tight for twenty minutes," he said. "I'll come back in my truck and get you."

"That isn't necessary. I can—"

"Just do it, okay? Go under that tree in the shade."

"Mitch, I'm perfectly capable of—"

"I know that! Humor me. I can't handle taking off when you're about to burst into tears. We're doing this my way!"

"You're pushy, Brannon!"

"Tough toasties, Star! Twenty minutes max. Don't move. And fix that damn dog's glasses. They're crooked."

Chelsey scowled after Mitch as he ran back across the field. Moments later she heard the roar of the powerful engine of the Ferrari, then the squeal of tires. She adjusted Zork's glasses and moved to sit under the tree.

She didn't have to stay here, she thought, crossing her arms over her breasts and blowing a large pink bubble. She could hike on home and be done with it. But it *was* awfully hot. Oh, who was she kidding? She wasn't about to budge until Mitch came back for her. It was really sweet of him to go all the way to his house to get his truck so Zork would fit. How many vehicles did Mitch own, for heaven's sake? He was strange. One minute he was yelling his head off about his windshield and the next thing she knew he was kind and thoughtful because she'd lost her bike. Playboys were a weird breed. And, oh, yes, he was a hustler, all right. Handsome, charming when he wasn't screaming, and definitely a megabucks boy.

Mitch Brannon was also, Chelsey decided, the most blatantly sexual man she had ever met. He literally oozed masculinity . . . was a veritable announcement of virility. And he knew it. Those long steady gazes he'd laid on her were not accidental. Mitch had his charisma routine down to a polished art and probably had to step over the bodies of the women who'd melted at his feet. She herself had not been unaffected by his sex appeal. There had been unsettling moments when she'd felt that pull, that magnetism of Mitch's, and it had been very disconcerting. She simply was not accustomed to a man having such an effect on her. Mitch Brannon was definitely dangerous!

But there she sat like a dingdong following his orders to the letter. Dumb. More than that, it was borderline bizarre. She was behaving like a starstruck teenager and she knew it. She really should start walking home. She wasn't going to, though, and she knew that too. She'd wait for Mitch just like he told her to. The question was, why?

She shrugged and tossed the now stale gum into a trash barrel. Back to the real problem at hand. How in the heck was she going to pay for Mitch's windshield? She had just paid Richard's fall tuition at UCLA and she was dead broke. Richard's part-time job at a restaurant had covered the cost of his books and other supplies and he'd been awarded a scholarship for his dormitory fees for the year, but Chelsey's bank account was down to nothing and she had the second semester tuition money to come up with. Richard would graduate in June, but until then he was her responsibility.

Chelsey and Richard's mother, Bessie Star, had refused to touch a penny of her husband's insurance money when he had died of a sudden heart attack. She had placed the money in a college fund for Chelsey. During Chelsey's senior year at UCLA, Bessie had succumbed to cancer, leaving only enough cash to cover the large medical bills that had accumulated during her illness. Chelsey had been determined that Richard should also have the education he deserved and had financed his years at UCLA where he was majoring in accounting.

During the summer Richard worked two jobs to help with part of his bills and shared a small house with two other students while waiting to move back into the dormitory on campus. The love of his life was a pretty girl who understood his circumstances and was content with an occasional movie, long walks, and ice-cream cones.

Chelsey and Richard were close, cared deeply for each other, and the loss of their parents had forged an even stronger bond between them. Richard insisted on working as a busboy in a restaurant during the school year and Chelsey worried constantly that he was trying to do too much. Her job as a computer systems analyst paid well, but barely covered the cost of both her and Richard's expenses and certainly could not support such luxuries as windshields for Ferraris! Chelsey could only hope that the bill for the repair would not be exorbitant and that Mitch would agree to accept a small monthly payment. Very small, in fact.

And if Mitch refused? Even if she managed to secure a loan from a bank she'd never be able to make the installments. Damn, what a mess. Why did she have to hit a home run on the day Mitch parked his new car outside the fence? She had long since sold her own car to cover Richard's fees and simply did not have anything of value left. And to top it off, her wonderful bike, which was her only means of transportation, was gone forever. Oh, damn.

"I tell you, Zork," Chelsey said miserably, "some days it just doesn't pay to get out of bed. This is really the pits."

Zork thumped his tail on the ground, then resumed his snooze as Chelsey sighed and leaned her head back against the tree. She'd figure something out, she always did, but at the moment things were looking awfully bleak. Her future was suddenly precarious and resting in the hands of a total stranger. Chelsey had seen Mitch both angry and compassionate, but the circumstances had been unusual, extreme. Actually, she knew absolutely nothing about him. So why was she sitting there waiting for a man who could be a sex maniac for all she knew? Because she wanted to, that's why. Great. That kind of reasoning could get her killed! Mitch could throw her into his truck and ravish her! No, he wouldn't do that. He was scared to death of her bespectacled horse. He didn't know that Zork wouldn't hurt a flea. But it wasn't because she had an enormous dog that Chelsey felt comfortable about going with Mitch. She trusted him. She didn't know why, but she did. He threw her senses off balance, occasionally rendered her incapable of thinking straight, but she trusted him.

Chelsey stared off into space as she recalled the sensations that had swept through her when Mitch had pulled her into his arms. She had felt protected and totally feminine and it had been heavenly. It had been no more than a comforting gesture on his part, but she had reacted to it as a woman would to a man's loving embrace. Not bright, but then her body had been behaving rather strangely ever since she had gotten her first glimpse of Mitch Brannon. The trick would be to keep her mind in control of the situation and not fall prey to Mitch's sensuality. She could handle that. No problem.

A late model maroon pickup truck pulled into the parking lot and Mitch stepped out and motioned to Chelsey. She nudged Zork and they started quickly across the field.

"Will he ride in the back," Mitch said as they approached, "or does he insist on driving?"

Chelsey rolled her eyes and patted the side of the bed of the truck. Zork immediately jumped in and calmly sat down. Chelsey turned to open the passenger door and saw the inscription, BRANNON CONSTRUCTION, painted on the side.

"I really appreciate your coming back like this, Mitch," she said as she slid onto the seat and closed the door.

"I wasn't sure you'd be here because of the way I barked at you," he said, smiling at her.

"I don't blame you for being in a rotten mood. I didn't exactly brighten your day."

"Oh, it wasn't a total loss," he said, turning the key in the ignition and backing out. "Which way?"

She gave him the directions to her house and then looked around the interior of the cab of the truck. The seats were plush and comfortable and an expensive-appearing CB unit hung below the dashboard.

Mitch drove the truck with relaxed ease through the winding, tree-lined streets of the residential area. The homes were small, some nicely kept, others obviously suffering from neglect.

"You're in construction?" Chelsey asked pleasantly.

"Partly. It's actually Brannon Development Company, but we do some of our own building."

"We?"

"My father, brother, and I."

"A family business? I think that's nice."

"Why?"

"Well, because some social analysts would have us believe that close-knit families are a thing of the past and it's refreshing to hear that there's still some left around."

"What about you, Chelsey? Do you belong to someone?"

"My brother, Richard."

"No one else?"

"Nope."

"You're really very pretty. I'm surprised there isn't a special man."

Chelsey laughed. "They're all afraid of my dog."

"I can see why," Mitch said. "That is one huge animal. So, are you looking for Mr. Right?"

"Looking? No, I'm waiting for Prince Charming."

"In this liberated society? Shame on you, Chelsey Star! You should go out and snag yourself a good catch."

"I flunked liberation," she said, grinning. "It's not my cup of tea. The whole thing seems kind of nuts."

"Really?" He looked over at her quickly. "Does that mean your brother watches over you?"

"Oh, no. I'm completely on my own. Richard is at UCLA."

"You're an unliberated woman who's all alone with no one to take care of you?"

She shrugged. "That about sizes it up."

"You're confusing me."

"Don't worry about it. I don't make much sense to myself sometimes either."

"I think you're an interesting, complicated woman, Chelsey."

"Not really. I just do what I have to do."

"Like impersonating Reggie Jackson?" he asked, chuckling.

"I won't do *that* again! There's my house. That funny little one tucked in between those others."

"Do you own it?" Mitch asked, pulling into the narrow driveway.

"Heaven's, no. I fixed it up myself, though. The landlord bought the materials and took my labor off the rent. My next project is the roof."

"The roof!" he exclaimed.

"It leaks." She opened her door and slid out, which was a signal to Zork to leap out of the truck bed. "Want to come in for a cool drink?"

Mitch scowled up at the roof, then followed Chelsey across the neatly trimmed lawn and in the front door.

"Come here, Zork," Chelsey said, pulling off the dog's sunglasses. "Find Myrtle."

"Myrtle?" Mitch asked.

"The cat. She's deaf, so Zork hunts her up so she knows we're home."

"I'm surprised you didn't get her a hearing aid."

"I thought of it, but she's stone deaf so it wouldn't have helped."

"I was kidding!"

"Well, I wasn't! Iced tea or lemonade?"

"Whatever you're having."

"Make yourself at home. I'll be right back," Chelsey said.

Mitch settled himself on the faded sofa and glanced around the small, immaculate room. Hardwood floors glistened in the sunlight and a multitude of plants were set on the floor in attractive groupings. An old-fashioned rocker was covered with a brightly patterned cushion and a small coffee table was in front of the sofa.

"Lemonade," Chelsey said, coming back into the room and handing Mitch a frosty glass. She sat down in the rocker and added, "Homemade, in fact, from lemons off the tree in the backyard."

"Thank you. You did a nice job in here, Chelsey."

"Would you believe someone had painted these floors? There must have been six layers of paint on them. It was a terrible mess."

"And you stripped them yourself?"

"Sure, and buffed my little heart out. Zork and Myrtle slip around a lot, but I think the floors are prettier all shiny and back to their natural state."

"Your plants sure are healthy."

"They better be! They're camouflaging the fact that I don't have much furniture." She laughed merrily.

"I didn't see a car in your driveway."

"I don't have one anymore."

"Chelsey, this doesn't make sense. I mean . . . Hey, this place is really cute. It is! But I know for a fact that people in your field make good money. Why are you living in a house with a leaky roof?"

"I have some other obligations," she said quietly.

"Isn't your brother concerned that you're going to float away the next time it rains?"

"He doesn't know about the roof, but it's not that big a deal anyway. Richard has his hands full with his studies and his job. Besides, my little house is coming along great. You should have seen it when I moved in. Yuck. I could hardly get to the front door because of the weeds."

Mitch frowned. "I suppose you cleaned the yard up yourself."

"Sure. Zork supervised."

"But you're not liberated, right?"

"Nope. My mother was a very old-fashioned woman. I loved her, but, even more, I liked her and the things she believed in. She insisted I have a good education so I could take care of myself if need be, but . . . well, I can't see making a big hoopla over counting heads and being sure there's enough women on the payroll and all that stuff. Token hiring isn't worth a hill of beans anyway, so what's the point? Equal pay for equal work is something else, though."

Before Mitch could reply, Zork suddenly appeared in the room with a furry black cat hanging sideways out of his mouth. Mitch's eyes widened and he choked on his lemonade, causing Chelsey to jump to her feet and pound him vigorously on the back.

"Good Lord!" Mitch said, gasping. "Your horse is eating the cat!"

Two

"Don't be silly." Chelsey laughed. "He always carries Myrtle around like that. She loves it. Zork, put her down. You're upsetting Mitch."

Eager to please, Zork deposited Myrtle on Mitch's lap. The cat yawned leisurely, Zork wagged his tail, and Mitch sneezed. And sneezed again.

"I'm allergic to cats," he said, staring at the bundle of fur.

"Oh, dear!" Chelsey snatched Myrtle up and carried her into the bedroom. "Are you all right?" she asked when she returned.

"Yeah, they just make me sneeze. Why does Zork haul her around in his mouth? That's really gross."

"I don't know, but they're great friends."

"And why is he staring at me?"

"Zork, go lie down! Don't you like pets, Mitch?"

"Well, sure, but yours are rather . . . unusual."

"A cat and a dog? Everyone has—"

Chelsey was interrupted by a squawking noise coming from a small box mounted on the wall. "Annie Oakley to OK Corral," a woman's squeaky voice said. "Come in, OK Corral."

"Excuse me," Chelsey said politely as Mitch's mouth dropped open. She pushed a button on the box. "This is the OK Corral," she said. "Go ahead, Annie."

"Buster is sitting over here, Chelsey. He's been waiting for you to get home."

"Send him on by," Chelsey said.

"Got it. Over and out."

" 'Bye, Annie."

Chelsey returned to her rocker and smiled at Mitch as if nothing out of the ordinary had taken place.

"You're waiting for me to ask, right?" he said, a puzzled frown on his face.

"Pardon me?"

"Okay, what the hell. Chelsey, why is Annie Oakley talking to you out of a box on your wall?"

"Oh, that. Well, her name is really Annie Franklin, but she thinks the other sounds classier over the wires. Anyway, she lives next door all alone and is crippled from arthritis. I worry about her so I rigged up an intercom system between the houses in case she needs me. Clever, huh?"

"Where's her family?"

"She doesn't have anyone but those of us in the neighborhood. She's so dear and I—oh, here's Buster."

"Who is Bus—"

"Come on in!" Chelsey called.

A short, round, bald man dressed in a pair of bib overalls lumbered in the door carrying a basket of vegetables.

"Howdy, Chelsey," he said.

"Hi, Buster. Meet Mitch. Mitch, this is Buster."

"Howdy," Buster said. Mitch nodded.

"So?" Chelsey said.

"Fresh ears of corn and white potatoes. You?"

"Tomatoes, radishes, cucumbers."

"Fair. I'll put these in your kitchen and go out back. I'll let myself out the gate."

"See ya, Buster." Chelsey waved breezily. "Would you care for some more lemonade, Mitch?"

"Huh? Oh, no thanks. Who was that guy? Farmer John?"

"Buster? Oh, we trade vegetables from our gardens so we don't get tired of eating the same things. That way Annie gets a variety too. It works out very nicely for everyone."

"It's a zoo around here," Mitch said, shaking his head. "You grow your own stuff?"

"Oh, yes, and bake bread. It really stretches the budget and it's delicious too."

"But why do you have to worry so much about what things cost when—"

"Chelsey! Are you home?" a voice called from the front porch.

"Sweet heaven," Mitch said, "now what?"

"Yes!" Chelsey yelled.

"Thank goodness," a tall, attractive dark-haired woman said, stomping into the room with a small suitcase in her hand. "Can I stay here tonight?"

"Sure." Chelsey nodded. "Polly, meet Mitch. Mitch, this is Polly."

"Hello," he said, raising his hand wearily.

"Gosh, did I interrupt something?" Polly said. "Ignore me. I'm going into the bedroom. Nice to have met you, Mitch. 'Bye. I swear, Chelsey, I'm not gonna take much more of this. Why can't she have sex in the back seat of a car like other people? It's too much. It really is."

"That was Polly," Chelsey said as the bedroom door slammed closed.

"Oh, really?"

"She has this roommate who's in love and keeps asking Polly to clear out so she can have the place to herself with her boyfriend so they can . . . you know."

"I've heard about it, yes. So Polly bunks in here?"

"She sleeps on the sofa. It's no bother."

"But what if you want to have someone in to . . . you know? Wouldn't it get a little crowded?"

"I don't . . . you know. You know what I mean?"

"Never?"

"Isn't this a little personal, Mitch?"

"Oh, yes, of course. I'm sorry. You could save a lot of time if you put a revolving door on this place. Chelsey, Zork is staring at me again."

"He likes you, Mitch."

"I've got to be going." Mitch stood up. "Thanks for the drink."

"And thank you for the ride. You'll be in touch about the windshield?" she asked, walking him to the door.

"Yep." He stopped and looked down at her. "You'll be hearing from me. Soon."

"I hope we can work out an agreement."

"I don't doubt it for a minute," he said, then tilted her chin up and kissed her. The kiss was sweet, soft, and incredibly sensuous, and Chelsey could hardly breathe. " 'Bye, Chelsey Star," Mitch said quietly, then turned and left the house.

" 'Bye," she whispered.

The truck roared into action and disappeared down the street. Chelsey didn't move.

"Can I come out now?" Polly asked.

"Huh? Oh, sure," Chelsey said, blinking several times.

"Goodness, Chelsey, who was that gorgeous man? What a specimen! I bet you could kill me for barging in on you."

"That's all right. He was here on business."

"I'd like to do business with that hunk. Did you say his name was Mitch?"

"Yes. I broke his windshield."

"Really? Why?"

"I hit a home run."

"No kidding? Just like Reggie Jackson. So was Mitch really mad?"

"It was a brand-new Ferrari."

"You're lucky to be alive, girl. You mean he has money to go along with that face and body?"

"I guess so," Chelsey said, sinking onto the rocker, "but I'm paying the repair bill."

"How?"

"I have no idea. I'm hoping Mitch will take monthly payments."

"You poor kid. As if you didn't have enough to take care of."

"Annie Oakley to OK Corral," the box squawked.

"I'll get it," Polly said. "Hi, Annie, this is Polly."

"Hello, sweetheart. Got thrown out again, huh? Who was the Golden Boy at Chelsey's?"

"His name is Mitch. He's beautiful," Polly said.

"Sure looked good from here. What's the scoop?"

"Nothing. Chelsey broke his windshield. It was all strictly business."

"Well, damn, forget it, then. Over and out."

Polly laughed. "Annie's all disappointed. Actually, so am I. You and Mitch look great together."

"I'm going to clean some corn," Chelsey said, getting up and heading for the small kitchen. "Oh, guess what? My bike was stolen."

"Oh, no! You've had a junky day. I'll help you with the veggies. Where did you lose your bike?"

"At the practice field. I was way on the other side waiting for Mitch to show up so I could explain about his windshield."

"Rotten. You were doing the honorable thing and some jerk cops your bike."

"I know. Mitch helped me look all over for it but it was long gone."

"That was nice of him, don't you think?"

"Yes, and then he went home for his truck so he could give me and Zork a ride."

"Class. The man has class, Chelsey. He also has so much sex appeal it's sinful. He's the kind of guy I leer at from a distance but would be scared to death to go out with."

"Why?"

"Chelsey, add it all up! Looks, build, money, that's the fast-lane crowd. The automatic end to an evening is a nice romp in the hay. That's how they say good night."

"Well, don't worry about it," Chelsey said, laughing

lightly. "The only time I'll see him again will be when he gives me the bill for his dorky car."

"Yeah, I suppose you're right. But, oh, Chelsey, he's so beautiful."

"Clean the corn, Polly."

After the two had scrubbed the vegetables Buster had delivered, Chelsey put Zork's sunglasses on him, collected Myrtle, and headed out to the backyard to work in the garden. Only then, in the solitude of the secluded yard, did Chelsey stop and place her fingertips on her lips.

It was as though Mitch had kissed her only moments before. Chelsey could still feel the warmth, the softness of his mouth as it had claimed hers. She recalled instantly the tingling sensation that had spread throughout her and the disappointment when Mitch lifted his head and ended the embrace.

What was it about that man? she thought. Oh, granted, he was different from anyone she had ever met, but that was no reason to turn into jelly whenever he looked at her. And that kiss! She had thought she would die on the spot. Why? Just because Mitch was handsome and well built didn't give him a corner on seduction. Why did she feel so strange when she was close to him?

She frowned. Come to think of it, he had no business kissing her at all! That was rather pushy. Delicious, but presumptuous. Goodness, Polly was right. If the Mitch Brannons of the world kissed women they didn't even know, then an evening on the town surely did end up in bed. So if she knew he was a hustler, why was she wasting her mental energies thinking about him and why did she react to his technique?

"Answer me that, Zork," Chelsey said. "Why do I transform into putty around Mitch Brannon? You don't know, huh? Well, my buddy, neither do I!"

She shook her head and turned back to the garden, firmly pushing the thought of Mitch from her mind. Later, she and Polly made a dinner of corn and hot dogs, plus the cheese and cookies Polly had brought along.

Polly flopped onto the sofa with a thick novel while Chelsey took a leisurely bath and shampooed her hair to prepare for her date with Tony Harrison. He was a fellow employee at the computer firm where she worked. Dressed in blue slacks and a light blue gauze blouse, her auburn hair a shiny cascade, Chelsey emerged from the bedroom to find Tony chatting with Polly.

"Hi, Chels," Tony said, getting to his feet. "Ready to go see a flick?"

"Sure. Polly, hold down the fort, okay?"

"Yep. Have fun, you two."

"You really should get a new roommate, Polly," Tony said.

"I know. The next one is going to be a nun!"

Tony walked to the box on the wall and pushed the button. "Hey, Annie, want us to leave the porch light on so you can watch me kiss Chelsey good night?" he asked.

"Stuff it, Harrison," Annie said. "Over and out."

Tony laughed. "You gotta love her. Take care of things, Zork."

Tony Harrison was a good-looking, trimly built tall man in his late twenties with dark hair and eyes and a tanned complexion. He would have preferred a more serious relationship with Chelsey, but when she had made it clear she wasn't interested, he had settled for being her friend and enjoying her company. Chelsey dated several other men as well, but had sent many packing when they had tried to rush her into bed. She was teased good-naturedly at work about waiting for her Prince Charming, and she would simply laugh and say that was exactly how it was.

And she meant it. Chelsey Star firmly believed that true love was one to a customer, winner take all. She had seen the beauty, the contentment of that type of commitment between her parents. As young as she had been when her father died, she could still remember the warm gazes, the gentle fleeting touches that had passed between the elder Stars. Oh, yes, Chelsey was waiting for her Prince Charming just as her mother had.

Chelsey had been looking forward to the evening out with Tony, but found she had difficulty concentrating on the movie. Before the lights had dimmed it had seemed as though every tall blond man in San Diego was in attendance. Chelsey watched them as they took their seats, dismissing them immediately as not being as handsome or as well built as Mitch Brannon. She was furious with herself for her behavior and ended up losing track of the plot of the film. Afterward, she and Tony went to a small café for coffee and pie.

"Are you all right, Chels?" Tony asked. "You're awfully quiet."

"I'm fine. How's that flight attendant you're seeing?"

"She's in Rome."

"Poor baby. Are you lonely?"

"Of course not! I'm with you! Except you're not here. What's wrong?"

"I . . . my bike got stolen today."

"No wonder you're bummed out. That was a great, old, ugly bike."

"I know. I also broke the windshield on a brand-new Ferrari. How's that?"

"Grim. How did it happen?"

"I hit a baseball over the fence at practice."

"Just like—"

"Yeah, Reggie Jackson."

On Chelsey's small front porch, Tony swept her dramatically into his arms, leaned her over backward, and placed a noisy kiss on her lips as Chelsey dissolved into laughter. He then stood her on her feet, saluted sharply in the direction of Annie's house, and bid Chelsey good night. Zork greeted her when she entered the house and she tiptoed through the living room, where Polly was camped out on the sofa. Zork picked Myrtle up in his mouth and followed Chelsey into the bedroom. He deposited Myrtle on the foot of the bed, flopped on the floor, and began to snore.

Once in bed, Chelsey stared up into the darkness. A wave of depression swept over her and a single tear slid down her cheek. She brushed it away angrily. She was suddenly so tired of struggling to make ends meet, living from paycheck to paycheck with nothing left over. There was only one more school year to go and then Richard would have achieved his goal, but it seemed like an eternity.

And now her precious bike was gone, and she had to pay for that damn windshield of Mitch's and—Mitch. There he was again in the front of her mind. Tall, strong, beautiful Mitch with his rich laughter and little boy smile. Mitch, who had kissed her so gently, so sweetly, she had nearly melted in his arms.

"Go away, Mitch Brannon," she said, punching her pillow. "Just leave me alone!"

The next morning, Chelsey leaned against the kitchen counter as she sipped a cup of coffee. She had not slept well and had had a mixed-up dream about a blond baseball player who was riding her old bike. She was dressed in her orange T-shirt that said COACH on the back and brown shorts. Her hair was tucked up under her baseball cap and she was not in a terrific mood.

Polly was still asleep when Chelsey left. She closed the door quietly behind her and headed in the direction of the playing field. Zork, plodding along happily beside her, was wearing his official bright orange sunglasses. They were his prestigious attire as the mascot for the Orange Crushers.

"Hey, coach," a voice boomed. "Want a ride?"

"Mitch!" Chelsey said, an instant smile on her face as he pulled his truck up to the curb. "What are you doing here?"

"I'm going to a baseball game. How about you?"

"You're planning to watch the Orange Crushers play?"

"Wouldn't miss it. Put your horse in the back and let's go. Snazzy glasses you've got there, Zork."

Zork was only too pleased to ride in the bed of the truck and Chelsey was still smiling when she climbed into the cab. Her gaze swept over Mitch's muscular form, which was outlined to perfection in faded jeans and a pale blue knit shirt. Her heart did its funny dance again, but she firmly ignored it.

"How did you know what time we were playing?" she asked as Mitch started down the street.

"I called the Parks and Recreation office. How's life in your calm abode?"

"Fine." She laughed. "I get the feeling my existence is not to your taste."

"I didn't say that. It just takes a little getting used to, I think. Is everyone doing okay? Annie, Polly, Buster, Myrtle, the whole group? Zork sure is dressed to kill today."

"Those are his Crusher sunglasses. He only gets to wear them to the games." Without pausing, she went on. "Mitch, why are you here? Did you get a price on the windshield?"

"No. I had to go into the office after I left you yesterday and today is Sunday, so . . . I wanted to see you, Chelsey, that's why I showed up this morning. It has nothing to do with my car."

"Oh, well, I . . ."

"Just say you're glad to see me too."

"It's a nice surprise, Mitch."

"Chelsey," he said quietly, "I couldn't get you out of my mind last night. Are—are you in some kind of trouble?"

"Trouble? What do you mean?"

"It doesn't add up, that's all. You're obviously very concerned about money and yet you have a lucrative job. I know it's none of my business, but—"

"No, it isn't," Chelsey said, frowning slightly, "but it's not a national secret. I'm helping put my brother through college. He has one more year to go and then everything will be fine. I had my chance because my mother insisted I have our father's insurance money for my college education. Now it's Richard's turn. He's working part-time which worries me sick because he's exhausted, but we're both hanging in there."

"Incredible," Mitch said, shaking his head. "You are something, Chelsey Star."

"Richard and I only have each other. We're very close.

You should be able to understand that because you come from a solid family. I'm sure you all work very hard at your business."

"That's true, we do."

"And wouldn't you help your brother or father or mother any way you could?"

"Of course."

"So we're not all that different, Mitch."

"Damn it, Chelsey, your roof leaks!"

"Oh, for heaven's sake." She laughed. "Are we back to that? I told you, I'm going to fix it."

"I don't want you crawling around on a roof! You could get hurt doing that! I thought you said you weren't liberated. Repairing a roof sounds pretty damn liberated to me!"

"What do you want me to do? Wave a magic wand?"

"No! You bake your bread and I'll fix the blasted roof!"

"Don't be silly."

"I mean it! When are you getting the supplies?"

"Next week, I think, but—"

"Then it's settled. The subject is closed."

"It certainly is not!" Chelsey said, poking him in the arm. "I'm getting money deducted from my rent for doing that work and I'm the one who is going to do it."

"No, you are not!"

"Don't push me, Brannon!"

"Shut up, Star! Bear in mind that I'm bigger than you are."

"Oh, wonderful! Now I get the macho routine." She crossed her arms over her breasts.

"That's right, sweetheart," Mitch said, grinning at her. "I'll win this one any way I can."

"Then I'll insist on paying you for your labor."

"Fine. It'll cost you a loaf of homemade bread."

Chelsey couldn't help laughing. "You're crazy."

"Probably. Is that your team all decked out in orange? Let's go play us a ball game, coach."

The Orange Crushers swarmed over Chelsey, Mitch, and Zork as they crossed the field and Chelsey raised her hands for silence.

"Hi, gang," she said. "This is my friend Mitch."

"What a bod," a freckle-faced girl said. "Are you a movie star?"

Mitch laughed. "No."

"Mitch owns that Ferrari with the broken windshield," Chelsey said.

"Aaak!" Patsy yelled, clutching her throat. "It's the hitman! We're dead meat!"

"Is she all right?" Mitch whispered to Chelsey.

"Patsy has a flair for the dramatic," she whispered back. "Patsy, Mitch is not going to shoot anyone. Tell her you're not a gangster, Mitch."

"Huh? Oh. Patsy, I solemnly swear that I am a very nice person."

"They all say that," Patsy said, sticking her nose in the air and stomping off.

"I tried," he said, shrugging.

"Hey, Chels!" Tony yelled, running up to the group.

"Hi!" Chelsey said. "Tony Harrison, this is Mitch Brannon."

"Brannon?" Tony said, shaking Mitch's offered hand. "As in Brannon Development?"

"Yes," Mitch said, nodding.

"You know each other?" Chelsey asked.

"Not directly," Tony said. "I was on the team that computerized Brannon Development about five years ago. We've expanded the system three times since. Your outfit is really going great guns, Brannon."

"We're holding our own," Mitch said quietly.

"Tony, are you the umpire today?" Chelsey asked.

"Yep. Should be a good game, Chels. The Maple Leafs are second to last and the Crushers are—"

"We know where we are, Tony. Are you wearing your contacts?"

"Chels, you know it's too dusty out here for my lenses."

"So where are your glasses?"

"Come on, Chels!"

"I'll yell foul, Tony! I won't have an umpire who's half blind!"

"Cripes! I'll get 'em," he said, heading back to his car. "Keep her under control, Brannon. She goes crazy at these things."

"Okay, Crushers," Chelsey said, clapping her hands. "Head for the bench. Thanks, Mitch," she added when she saw him carefully straightening Zork's orange glasses.

"Chels?" Mitch said as they walked across the field.

"Tony is the only one who calls me that," she said.

"You work together?"

"Yes, we're good friends."

"Friends?"

"Yes. Why?"

"Nothing. There's a pretty good crowd here."

"The parents are very supportive. Don't expect too much, Mitch. The Crushers are the leftovers."

"What do you mean?"

"Well, I went down to Parks and Recreation to look for an extra job for the summer. I thought I could teach a class on gardening or bread baking. Something like that. Anyway, these girls were cut from the other teams because they just didn't have the ability and there was a set number of positions available. There was only enough money to pay me half what the other coaches are getting and they gave us a catcher's mask, a bat, and a ball. That's it."

"And you stood still for that?"

"Hey, they didn't do so hot either. I know zip about baseball. *Nada.* But we've had a wonderful time, a lot of fun. I dyed their shirts orange so we'd sort of have uniforms and they had their own gloves."

"Okay, bald lady, let's see what they can do."

"I sure don't know what you have against my cap! It's a great cap! A regulation baseball cap! It has class, style, and—"

"Put a cork in it, Chelsey."

"Okay," she said cheerfully. "Play ball!"

An hour later, Mitch cringed and covered his eyes with his hand as Chelsey once again jumped up from the bench.

"Are you crazy, Harrison?" she shrieked. "A strike? Strike! Clean your glasses, ump!"

"Chels, I'm going to evict you from this game!" Tony roared. "Have you no respect? That was a clean strike!"

"Oh, ha! You wouldn't know one if you saw one."

"Sit!" Mitch said, grabbing Chelsey around the waist and plopping her back on the bench. "It was a strike."

"Really?" she said. "I'll be darned."

Mitch chuckled and shook his head, then absently scratched Zork's head as the huge dog began to doze off at his feet.

"This is the closest score we've ever had," Chelsey said, her eyes dancing with excitement as she rubbed her hands together.

"It's zero to zero!" Mitch said.

"Well, the Maple Leafs aren't ahead, are they?"

He laughed. "You've got a point there, coach. Hey, Patsy keeps looking at me like I'm an ax murderer."

"Ignore her. She must watch too much TV."

Mitch's glance fell on a pint-sized girl who was sitting on the ground drawing a picture in the dirt with a stick.

"What's her name?" Mitch said.

"Who? Oh, that's Cindy. She's so small for her age, but she tries hard. Poor kid, hasn't had a hit all season. You saw her at the plate. Three pitches, three swings, she's done."

"Mmm," Mitch said thoughtfully.

The game proceeded on course with Chelsey screaming at Tony, Tony threatening to throw her out, and Mitch hauling Chelsey back onto the bench. In the bottom of the ninth inning there was still no score.

"I'm a wreck," Chelsey said. "This is our last time at bat."

"Cindy is due up," Mitch said. "I'm going to talk to her a minute."

"Give her the old win-it-for-the-Gipper speech," Chelsey said.

Mitch hunched down next to the tiny girl and when Chelsey glanced at them, Cindy was nodding her head vigorously and smiling. When it was Cindy's turn to bat, she marched to the plate, wiggled her little bottom, and glowered at the pitcher.

"Oh, no," Chelsey said, "she's on the wrong side of the plate!"

"Trust me," Mitch said.

"But—"

Crack!

Cindy's bat connected with the ball and sent it sailing out into centerfield. The Crushers came off the bench and screamed their hearts out. Zork woke up with a jerk and barked at full volume as Cindy rounded the bases as fast as her spindly legs would carry her.

"Go for home plate!" Chelsey yelled as the ball was thrown to the catcher. "Oh! Oh! She made it! We have a run!"

"Aw right!" Mitch said, punching his fist in the air. "Way to go, Cindy!"

"I can't believe it!" Chelsey threw her arms around Mitch's neck. "What did you say to her?"

"Tell you later," he said, kissing her quickly on the lips.

Chelsey suddenly realized where her arms were and dropped them quickly to her sides. The game was over! The Orange Crushers now knew the sweet smell of victory! Bedlam broke loose as everyone hugged everyone and the parents descended on the field. Then tearful good-byes were exchanged as the team dispersed for the last time.

"I love you all," Chelsey called as the girls left the field.

"Nice game, coach," Tony said. "Congrats."

"Thanks, Tony. You called it fair and square."

"Always do, Chels. See you at work tomorrow."

" 'Bye, Tony."

"See ya, Brannon," Tony said.

"Yeah." Mitch nodded.

"Oh, Mitch, we won!" Chelsey said, sinking onto the bench. "I'm exhausted. Oh, what was the secret potion with Cindy?"

"I was watching her draw a picture in the dirt. The kid is left-handed, Chelsey. You had her batting right. I just switched her to the other side of the plate and socko! She hit it!"

"Lord, I'm a lousy coach." She laughed. "But you are wonderful. Thank you, thank you, thank you!"

"Glad I could be of serivce, ma'am. What do you say we go out to dinner tonight to celebrate? We'll get all dolled up and do it right."

"Dinner?"

"I want to be with you this evening, Chelsey," he said quietly.

"That—um—sounds lovely."

"I'll pick you up at seven. But I'll take you and Zork home now. I have to go to work."

"On Sunday?"

"We're in the middle of a big rush deal. We're all putting in overtime. We'll wrap it up in a few days."

In the truck, Mitch put the key in the ignition but did not turn it on. He just sat there, frowning.

"What's wrong?" Chelsey asked.

"Tony Harrison."

"What about him?"

"I can picture it now, Chelsey. He'll come running up to you at work tomorrow and tell you all about me."

"Are you awful? Heavens, you're not really a hitman, are you?"

"You've never heard of Brannon Development, have you?"

"No, should I have? I didn't do any of the computer analyzing for your company."

"Do you know where the Mountain View Shopping Plaza is?"

"Sure."

"The Rendondo Towers condos? The McGraw Sports Arena?"

"Yes, why?"

"We own them, and a lot of other things."

"And? What message am I missing here?" she asked.

"I'm a very wealthy man, Chelsey."

"So? What does that have to do with anything?"

"Well . . . nothing, I guess," he said, looking at her with an astounded expression on his face.

"Am I supposed to be impressed, awed? Why are we having this conversation, Mitch?"

"I really don't know." He shook his head. "It's just been so long since a woman said 'Hi, Mitch,' and not 'Hi, Money.' They look at me and see dollar signs. I never met anyone like you before, Chelsey."

"The fact that you pay more taxes than I do has nothing to do with me, Mitch. You are you, and I am me, I mean I. Very simple. Let's go to my house and have some lemonade. I hope Polly is awake."

Mitch suddenly leaned across the seat and pulled Chelsey's baseball cap off. As the tousled auburn hair fell about her shoulders, he gently ran his fingers through it. Then, cupping her face in his large hands, he claimed her mouth in a long, sensuous kiss, parting her lips and flickering his tongue against hers. An ember of desire started glowing deep within Chelsey and warmth traveled throughout her body. She circled Mitch's neck with her arms and urged him closer. The kiss intensified as Mitch drew her hard against him, crushing her breasts against his solid chest.

"I like you, Chelsey Star," he said finally, his voice husky. "I like you a helluva lot."

"I like you, too, Mitch Brannon," she said breathlessly, willing her heart to stop racing. "Want some lemonade?"

"I never pass up homemade lemonade." He smiled, then moved away from her and started the truck.

Chelsey hoped she sounded halfway intelligent during the short drive to her house. The passionate kiss she had shared with Mitch had left her physically and emotionally shaken. She had responded to him with such total abandon it had been almost frightening. And the worst part was, she hadn't wanted that kiss to end! She could have sat there all day relishing the feel of Mitch's sensuous lips, his strong but gentle hands, his enticing aroma, his— She had to get a grip on herself! She had never, ever reacted to a man in such a manner. Desire had swirled within her and she had been powerless to control it.

What if she succumbed to Mitch's charms and sensual expertise? She'd hate herself, and him! She was waiting for her Prince Charming, dammit, and was not hopping into bed with anyone else in the meantime! Mitch apparently found her attractive, but Chelsey wasn't kidding herself. He was used to glamorous women who moved in the fast lane and were comfortable with casual sex and physically gratifying short-term relationships. He was momentarily fascinated by her unusual existence and whacko friends, and was hanging around to see what would happen next in her funny little house.

She must not, she told herself firmly, read more into his attentiveness than was actually there. And, heaven help her, she must absolutely not lose sight of who she was and what her values and principles were. Mitch was waking up her slumbering femininity and desires she didn't know she possessed, and she was going to put them back to sleep! He came from a different world, a lifestyle beyond her comprehension, and was definitely out of her league. She would go out to dinner with him, make arrangements to pay for his windshield, and that would be that. No more Mitch Brannon.

It was sound, sensible reasoning. So why was the thought of never seeing him again so depressing? Why did she miss him already when he was sitting right next to her in the truck? What in the hell was the matter with her? Her noble statements regarding the unimportance of Mitch's wealth had been sincere. It really didn't matter how much money he had, or which social circles he moved in. It had no significant bearing on her and Mitch as a couple because they weren't one! Deep within her Chelsey knew it. And deep within her that made her incredibly sad. .

"Safe and sound," Mitch said, pulling into Chelsey's driveway. "I swear, that dog can sleep anywhere. He's zonked back there."

"Baseball games wear him out," Chelsey said, opening her door. "He gets very emotionally involved."

"He slept through half of it! I kept having to shove his glasses back on his nose because his snoring was shaking them off. Actually, I don't think orange is his color. I decided that around the fourth inning."

"Oh, really?" Chelsey laughed as she slid out of the cab. "Maybe I should name my next team the Purple Passions."

"Catchy," Mitch said as Chelsey wiggled Zork's tail to wake him up. "Hey, your roofing supplies are here."

"Is that what that stuff is?" She walked over to the pile sitting on the lawn.

"Yeah, and if you touch it, I'll wring your pretty little neck."

"I'm not afraid of you."

"You should be, because I mean it, Chelsey." Mitch frowned. "I'm not even going to be polite about it. You simply are not going up on that roof."

"Whatever." She shrugged. "If you're dumb enough to fix it for a loaf of bread, who am I to argue with you? Have a wonderful time."

"You really aren't hung up on this liberation junk, are you?"

"I told you I wasn't."

"But you're so darn self-sufficient and independent at times that I can't figure out where you're coming from."

"Don't boggle your mind about it, Mitch. Let's go have some lemonade. Come on, Zork, go find Myrtle."

"But don't bring her to me!" Mitch yelled.

In a few minutes they were seated on the sofa in the living room with their drinks. "Polly put a pot of vegetable soup on to simmer before she left," Chelsey said. "Want to stay for lunch?"

"I can't. I really have to get to the office."

"Forget my silly roof until you have time. I know you're very busy."

"What if it rains?"

"I put the plants under the drips. They just slurp up the water."

"Annie Oakley to OK Corral," the box squawked.

"My turn," Mitch said, walking to the wall. "Hi, Annie," he said after pushing the button.

"That you, Golden Boy?"

"Golden Boy?" Mitch whispered.

"That's what she calls you," Chelsey whispered.

He chuckled. "Yep, Annie, it's me."

"How'd the Orange Crushers do?"

"We won. One to zip."

"Hot damn! About time. Well, go back to kissing Chelsey."

"Think I should?"

"Absolutely, but don't do none of that fancy nonsense like that Harrison kid. I've got faith in you, Golden Boy. Over and out."

" 'Bye, Annie," Mitch said.

"I think I'll take Annie some soup," Chelsey said.

"Back up here. What's this bit about Harrison and his fancy kissing?"

"He was just being silly because he knew Annie was watching out the window."

"When?"

"Last night."

"You were with Harrison last night?"

"We went to the movies. What are you? A member of the FBI? Why all the questions, Mitch?"

"I thought you said you two were just friends."

"We are! What's the matter with you?"

"I have no idea." He slouched onto the sofa. "I sound like a jealous lover. I'm sorry."

"You're forgiven."

"I have to kiss you now, Chelsey."

"You do?"

"Of course. Annie told me to and I was raised to respect my elders and not question their directives."

"Oh." She went over to the sofa and into the reach of Mitch's outstretched arms.

The Brannons certainly had produced a well-mannered son, Chelsey thought dreamily as she was gathered into Mitch's embrace. He kissed her eyes and nose and cheeks, then claimed her mouth to seek and find her tongue. Chelsey fanned her fingers out over the broad expanse of Mitch's back and felt the muscles bunch under her touch. His mouth left hers and traveled down the slender column of her throat, and she leaned her head back slightly to give him greater access. Again he took possession of her mouth in a searing kiss that left her trembling when he lifted his head.

"Tonight. Seven," he said quietly, then released her.

"Yes," was all she managed to say.

" 'Bye, babe." He pushed himself to his feet and left the house.

Chelsey drew a shaky breath and pressed her hands to her flushed cheeks. She was definitely in trouble. Each time Mitch touched, and held, and kissed her, she responded with more intensity, giving more of herself. She was unable to stop from falling under the magical spell he cast over her mind, her reasoning, her body. He had jogged into her life on his long legs, hollered his head off because she'd broken his windshield, and now had kissed the living daylights out of her. What was next? Mitch wasn't a naïve kid. Surely he was aware of her increased response each time he kissed her. Was she falling prey to a well-executed seduction?

But why should he bother? He could be with a woman who owned a penthouse apartment and drove a car as flashy as the Ferrari. A man like Mitch could have been cruising on a yacht today, but had chosen to watch a bunch of little girls play baseball. His blue eyes had danced with excitement when Cindy made the run, as if he really cared whether or not the Crushers won. He had even allowed Zork to sleep on his foot!

"You confuse me, Mitch Brannon," Chelsey said. "You really, really do."

Three

The depositing of Myrtle onto her lap by Zork brought Chelsey out of her troubled reverie and she gave the cat a noisy kiss on the end of her nose. The trio headed for the garden after Chelsey had eaten a bowl of Polly's delicious vegetable soup and delivered a container full to Annie. Chelsey enjoyed her peaceful hours working in the soil and the thriving rows of vegetables gave evidence of her careful attention.

Several hours later, she was blow-drying her thick hair in front of the mirror. She leaned closer and peered at her reflection. Definitely not glamorous, she decided, but she was attractive, pretty, in fact. Compared to whom? High society women with their perfect hairdos and makeup? No, they were on a different plane, in a place of their own where Chelsey wouldn't fit in or feel comfortable. So why was Mitch Brannon wasting his time with her? Why was he stepping out of the world where he belonged and seeking her out? What did he want from her?

But more than that, she thought, what was she hoping to find in Mitch Brannon? Nothing? Everything? Her Prince Charming? That was ludicrous! Mitch wasn't seriously interested in her! The kisses and tender embraces that were turning her into a dimwit were probably ordinary occurrences for him. He had it all; looks, build, money. He had probably charmed his way into half the bedrooms in San Diego. Oh, that was nasty. But Mitch was obviously no candidate for the priesthood. That was one gorgeous hunk of stuff and women were not idiots. They knew a good thing when they saw it and Mitch was definitely a good thing!

"So why me, I ask you?" Chelsey said to the mirror. "It's not because the man is crazy about my dog!"

Her small wardrobe produced a choice of three dresses appropriate for the evening and she selected a pale green one with a filmy over-skirt. It had spaghetti straps, the neckline scooped to the top of her full breasts, and the skirt fell in soft folds to midcalf. Her thin strapped evening sandals accentuated her shapely legs and a narrow belt nipped in at her tiny waist. She dabbed cologne behind her ears, added a light rose gloss to her lips, and decided she looked splendid. Her dark eyes were sparkling with excitement and she knew it wasn't because she was being treated to a fancy dinner. She was spending the next few hours with Mitch Brannon and the thought was exhilarating. Dangerous, but exhilarating.

The knock at the door at precisely seven o'clock brought Chelsey instantly to her feet to answer it.

"Hello," Mitch said as he stepped into the room. "You—Chelsey, you look beautiful."

"Thank you. So do you." Oh, he was just too much! she thought wildly. Tan, perfectly cut suit with a dark brown shirt and tie. Absolutely devastating!

"Ready to go?" he asked.

"I just have to put my crew out. Zork, get Myrtle."

With the animals safely in the backyard, Chelsey picked up her clutch purse and proceeded Mitch out the front door. Her nostrils picked up the aroma of his musky aftershave.

"A different car?" she asked as Mitch assisted her into a plush automobile.

"It's my brother's. I didn't want to go in a truck."

"Please don't remind me that your Ferrari is wounded."

"My lips are sealed."

He started the car, tuned the radio to a station that played dreamy music, and pulled out into the street.

"Is your brother older or younger than you?" Chelsey asked.

"Mike is thirty-eight and I was thirty-five last week."

"Last—oh, no! You bought yourself that car to celebrate your birthday! Oh, Mitch, I feel so terrible."

"We're not discussing it, remember?" he said, smiling.

"Well, happy birthday," she said miserably.

"Thank you. My mom put thirty-five candles on my cake. I thought she was going to burn the house down."

"You had a party?"

"Just family. We've had this tradition since we were kids where we get to pick the menu for our birthday dinner. I called up my mom and placed my order."

"How marvelous! What did you have?"

"Fried chicken, potato salad, baked potatoes, and French fries."

"Isn't that an awful lot of potatoes?"

"I love 'em. Rule is everyone has to eat it with no complaints. It gets grim sometimes. Last year my father had watermelon."

"And?"

"That's it! Just a table full of watermelon. Mike and I snuck out later and went to McDonald's. We were starving!"

"Your family sounds so nice, Mitch."

"They're a good group. My mom is no bigger than you are, but we never cross her. She's tough and I love her. She's a pushover for her grandchildren, though. Mike has two little girls that are dolls. Man, they are so cute. Do you like babies, Chelsey?"

"Yes."

"Are you going to have a couple someday?"

"Probably not," she said quietly.

"No?"

"I have some very definite ideas on motherhood that don't mesh with the economy."

"What do you mean?" He looked at her as he stopped at a red light.

"I want to stay home and raise my children, not leave them in a day-care center. Very few women have that luxury now because of the spiraling costs of everything. It would break my heart to leave my baby and go to work, so I really don't think I'll ever have a child."

"You'd chuck your career to tend to a home and family?" he asked, pressing on the gas pedal as the light turned green.

"It's a job, not a career. Those computers have lost their charm. I'm actually bored out of my mind, but it pays well. Maybe I'll try something else once Richard graduates."

"Like what?"

"I have no idea." She laughed. "Maybe I'll become a professional baseball coach."

"I wouldn't recommend it."

"No? Well, darn."

Their mingled laughter danced through the car, the enclosure seeming to snatch up the delightful resonance and toss it playfully from corner to corner until the automobile overflowed with the joyous sound. A few minutes later Mitch turned into the parking lot of a well-known, expensive restaurant and came around to open Chelsey's door.

Great puffs of cumulus clouds dotted the sky, as though someone had blown across the top of a mug of hot chocolate, spraying fluffy whipped cream in all directions. Then Mother Nature had dipped her paint-brush in to hues of purple, orange, and yellow and transformed the horizon into a celebration of color and beauty.

"What a lovely sunset," Chelsey said. "I never get tired of seeing them."

"Sometimes I get too busy to look," Mitch said, gazing up at the sky.

"You work too hard."

"I'll tell my father you said so." He chuckled. "We'll threaten to turn Zork loose on him if he doesn't lighten up. I told Mike about Zork's glasses and he wouldn't believe me and asked if I had been drinking. I swore to him I was telling the truth and he told me to go take a nap and see if I felt better. It was very frustrating."

"Oh, my," Chelsey said, laughing.

They entered the restaurant and the maître d' greeted them immediately. "Mr. Brannon," he said, "how delightful to see you. Are you meeting your parents?"

"They're here? No, I have a separate reservation. We'll join them for a drink though, if you'll hold my table."

"Of course. I'll show you where they are seated."

Oh . . . good . . . grief! Chelsey thought. Mitch's mother and father?

"This is great," Mitch said. "You can meet my folks."

"Lovely," she said, forcing a smile.

Frank Brannon was an older version of Mitch with the same build and clear blue eyes. His hair was silver-gray and his suit had an expensive sheen to it. Kathleen Brannon was small and delicate and wore a pale pink silk dress. Her hair was also gray and had obviously been professionally styled. As she said her polite hellos and sat down, Chelsey felt like someone who had selected her attire at a rummage sale.

"Why don't you eat with us, Mitch?" Kathleen said. "We've just ordered."

"No, thanks, Mom. Chelsey and I are celebrating and I want her all to myself."

"What's the occasion?" Frank asked. "We already suffered through your potato birthday."

"Chelsey's Little League team won their game today."

"You coach baseball?" Kathleen said.

"Well, I . . . sort of," Chelsey said, deciding she would rather be at the dentist's than sitting at that table. "Mitch saved the day because I had a left-handed batter all backward. I really didn't know what I was doing."

"But I bet you had fun," Kathleen said, smiling warmly. "That's what counts. When Mike and Mitch played football I would go and scream and yell. It was grand."

"She was a wild woman at those games," Frank said. "I just groaned when both boys decided to play all through college. I didn't think I'd survive it."

"Chelsey held her own," Mitch said. "I wouldn't have given you a nickel for that umpire's life today and he was a friend of hers!"

"Good for you, Chelsey," Kathleen said.

Mitch smiled warmly at Chelsey as the drinks were served and she found herself relaxing. Kathleen Brannon went crazy at her sons' football games? What fun. How normal.

"Excuse me, Mr. Brannon," a waiter said. "Telephone call for you, sir."

A telephone was placed on the table and Frank picked up the receiver.

"Yes? Yes, he is," he said. "Oh? . . . You don't say . . . Well, I'll certainly look into it."

As he hung up the phone, Frank burst into laughter, causing the others to look at him in surprise.

"Frank?" Kathleen said.

"That was Mike," he said, wiping tears of merriment from his eyes. "Apparently you told him you were coming here, Mitch, and your mother had mentioned we were too."

"So?" Mitch said. "What's his problem?"

"He said to check your pockets for funny cigarettes because you had been ranting on about a Great Dane that wears sunglasses whenever he goes out."

"Mike called to tell you that? My brother is nuts," Mitch growled.

"I believe he thinks *you* are," Frank said, dissolving in a fit of laughter again.

"Chelsey," Mitch said, "tell them about Zork, will you?"

"Who?" Chelsey said.

"Your dog! With the glasses! My family is about to have me committed or run in on drug charges."

"Dog?" She looked at him with an innocent expression on her face. "I have a cat named Myrtle that makes you sneeze, but—"

"Chelsey, don't do this to me!"

"It was awfully hot at that game today, Mr. Brannon," Chelsey said to Frank. "One could fry one's brain if one wasn't careful."

"Mom," Mitch said, "listen to me, okay? Chelsey has a Great Dane named Zork, who has eye problems so he wears sunglasses. This morning they were orange because of the Crushers and . . . Mom?"

"You'll be all right, dear," Kathleen said, smiling sweetly and patting his hand. "We'll get you the finest doctors in the country."

"That does it!" Mitch said, getting to his feet and grabbing Chelsey's arm. "Good-bye, Mr. and Mrs. Whoever You Are."

"It was a pleasure to meet you, Chelsey," Kathleen said.

"I love it. I love it," Frank said, still chuckling. "Have a nice dinner."

"Good night," Chelsey said, as Mitch practically lifted her off her feet and hustled her to their table on the opposite side of the room.

"Hi!" she said when they were seated.

"Don't speak to me, Chelsey."

She laughed. "Okay."

"Why is it that you're the one with the weird dog and I'm the one everybody thinks is crazy?"

"I don't know." She shrugged. "Your parents are certainly lovely people."

"You all deserve each other—Mike included. I'm the only sane member of the group. I'm going to tell him, you know."

"Who?"

"Zork. He's got the right to know that you pretended he didn't exist. It's going to blow his mind."

"Zork who?"

"Oh, man." Mitch laughed. "You are so cuckoo and I adore you, Chelsey Star. Life with you is never, ever dull."

"That's true."

"My folks really liked you. I could tell."

"They're marvelous. Your house must have rung with laughter when you were growing up."

"Yes, it did. It's still wild when we all get together."

"Does your mother work at your company?"

"No. She always said her family was her career."

"She's very fortunate."

"There are still families like that, Chelsey, where the mother is a . . . mother."

"Not in my neighborhood."

"Maybe not, but—"

"Would you care to see the menu now, sir?" the waiter asked.

The meal passed with friendly banter, comfortable conversation, and discoveries. Chelsey pressed Mitch for more information on his childhood and he related outrageous stories of his and Mike's antics. They exchanged memories of their college days, and Mitch said he hadn't been that great a football player but was dashingly handsome in the snazzy uniform. It was fun, and Chelsey felt more alive, young, and carefree than she had since she could remember. She basked under the warm, tender gazes Mitch gave her and matched him smile for smile as they ate their delicious dinner. When the senior Brannons had an expensive bottle of wine sent to their table, Mitch raised his glass in a toast and told Chelsey she had definitely made a hit with his parents.

Chelsey felt like Cinderella. She had been turned into a lovely princess and transported to a fairy-tale land where everything glittered and there were no worries. But like Cinderella, she knew she would have to go back to her real world at the end of the night. Was it possible that Mitch *was* the Prince Charming she'd been waiting for? she wondered as the waiter poured fresh coffee. Or would he disappear when the clock struck twelve? If only she knew what Mitch wanted from her. She was tee-tering on the edge of new, strange sensations and emotions whenever she was with him. What if she fell? What heartache might she bring into her life if she fell in love with Mitch Brannon?

"Good food and beautiful company," Mitch said as he finished his coffee. "I'd better get you home since there's work tomorrow. How do you get there if you don't have a car?"

"The bus. Well, two buses actually. I transfer halfway across town."

"Where do you catch it?"

"About a half-mile from my house."

"Dammit, Chelsey, that's lousy."

"It's good exercise."

"What if it rains?"

"I do own an umbrella, Mitch."

"Blowing rain."

"I get wet."

"I'm hating this," he said, frowning. "You're playing out a bad hand and it stinks."

"Nope. I'm doing fine."

"Are you?" he asked softly. "Are you really?"

"Yes, Mitch, I am."

"I worry about you, Chelsey."

"Mitch, you hardly know me."

"Oh, that's not true. No, pretty Chelsey, that's not true at all. Shall we go?"

A twinkling array of stars shone in the summer sky as they walked to the car. Once seated in it, Mitch smiled and extended his hand. Without hesitation Chelsey moved next to him and he circled her shoulders with his arm while he steered the car with his other hand. Neither spoke in the comfortable silence as soft music from the radio drifted around them. Mitch suddenly chuckled and Chelsey looked up at him questioningly.

"This just proves that something good comes from everything that happens," he said. "If we were in the Ferrari you'd be stuck over there in a bucket seat. This is much nicer."

"Had to mention that car, didn't you?" Chelsey said, poking him in the ribs. "Are you taking it to the repair shop tomorrow?"

"I might not have time. I'm on a tight schedule right now, you know."

"Oh. I hope you can get it done soon, though. I'll feel a lot better when we've worked out a payment schedule of some kind."

"Yeah, well, we'll see. They might not carry windshields for Ferraris in stock. Don't worry about it, Chelsey. I'll let you know what happens."

"But it was your birthday present to yourself and—"

"Shhh. Enough on the subject."

When they arrived at her house Chelsey handed Mitch her key.

"Wave good night to Annie," she said, waggling her fingers in the direction of the neighboring house. Mitch blew Annie a kiss.

"Okay, where's the back door?" he said, shrugging out of his jacket when they entered the living room. "I'm talking to Zork."

"Through the kitchen," Chelsey said. "Would you like some coffee?"

"Sure."

When Mitch opened the back door Zork padded in with Myrtle in his mouth and wagged his tail in an enthusiastic greeting. While Chelsey stayed in the kitchen to prepare the coffee, Mitch disappeared into the living room with the animals. Chelsey giggled her way through the entire conversation that she overheard.

"Zork," Mitch said, "put Myrtle down. No, not on me! Over there. Okay, listen, pal. Chelsey finked out on you. She cracked under the pressure and claimed she'd never heard of you. I know it's hard to take, but you'll have to toughen up. Why are you smiling? This is serious, Zork. Don't go to sleep on my foot! Oh, for Pete's sake!"

"Here we are," Chelsey said, carrying a tray to the coffee table and sitting down next to Mitch. "Did Zork disown me?"

"He laughed. He did! He got a big, silly grin on his face."

"I guess he's going to stick by me no matter what I do."

"Smart horse," Mitch said softly, pulling Chelsey into his arms.

He placed a ribbon of kisses down her throat, then took possession of her mouth. His tongue flickered over her lips, parting them, meeting her tongue as the kiss intensified. Chelsey leaned into him, circling his neck with her arms and inching her fingers into his thick blond hair. His hands slid to her full breasts, his thumbs trailing over them, bringing the taut buds to throbbing awareness. She trembled under the onslaught of his maddening touch and a soft moan escaped her as he continued to kiss her, his questing tongue exploring each secret place within her mouth.

Desire surged unchecked within her and as Mitch eased the straps off her shoulders, she lifted her arms to free herself of the restricting material. Her breasts pushed above her scant bra, and he drew a ragged breath as his gaze roamed over the nearly bare ivory mounds.

"Beautiful," he said. "Like velvet, soft velvet."

Her bra seemed to float away and he leaned her back against the throw pillows. Chelsey's hands were shaking as she tugged his tie loose and undid the buttons on his shirt, her fingers sinking into the tawny curly hair on his chest. Mitch lowered his head and kissed her breasts, and she gasped as he drew first one and then the other rosy bud into his mouth.

Everything seemed surrounded by a rosy glow of euphoria. Time, space, reality, and reason stopped. Chelsey's passion grew as the ember was kindled into a raging flame of desire that swept through her. Nothing was important but the moment and this man. Her body ached for him, wanted to have what his masculinity and power and strength were promising. As he leaned against her she could feel the evidence of his arousal and rejoiced in the knowledge that she had excited him, made him desire her as she did him.

"Oh, Chelsey," he murmured, "I want you so much. So much."

Her name, Mitch's voice, they were real. They brought back the room, the sofa, Zork sleeping on the floor. Oh, damn, Chelsey thought, swallowing the sob in her throat. The clock had chimed and Cinderella was home.

"Mitch, no," she whispered. "Oh, I'm sorry. I should never have let you . . ."

Mitch slowly sat up, then helped her pull her dress back into place. He buttoned his own shirt with visibly shaking hands as he took a shuddering breath. He wiped a line of perspiration off his forehead with his thumb.

"I know you're angry," she said quietly. "It wasn't fair. I led you to believe I was willing to . . . I'm so sorry."

"I guess I was pretending it wasn't true, but I knew it was," he said, turning to look at her.

"What do you mean?"

"You've never been with a man. I could tell that from things you've said. I want you so much. I just—I'm the one who is so sorry, Chelsey. I won't take that from you. It's too precious. It's a treasure, a gift."

"I told you I flunked liberation, Mitch," she said, blinking back her tears. "I'm very glad I met you, though, and—"

"Dammit, Chelsey, are you dusting me off?"

"Well, why would you hang around if—"

"Thanks a helluva lot!" he yelled. "Is that what you think of me? I won't be interested if you don't go to bed with me? What am I? A sex maniac? Well, I guess I acted like one, but, dammit, I won't stand for this! You make me smile and laugh, Chelsey, and you drive me nuts, and you're wonderful. I looked at a sunset tonight because you were there. I want to see you and be with you and—"

"Why are you hollering at me?"

"I'm not! Yes, I am. Look at that dog. He slept through the whole thing. Chelsey, do you want me to get out of your life and leave you alone?"

"I—no, I don't."

"Good."

"But . . ."

"We'll take it slow and easy, I promise. There won't be a repeat performance of tonight."

"Mitch, I have to say this. You didn't force yourself on me. I wanted you to kiss me, touch, and hold me. I've never felt like that before. I'm not sorry it happened. You made me feel alive, feminine, special. It wasn't fair to you to call a halt like that, but for me it was so new and wonderful."

"Oh, man, you're killing me. I knew you were responding to me. But don't do it, Chelsey. Don't give your gift to me. Save it for your Prince Charming."

"Oh, Mitch."

"I'm not a saint. I wanted you, Chelsey. I still do. I should walk out of here and go back to the floozies, but I can't. God help me, I can't."

"I think we're in a heap of trouble here," Chelsey said miserably.

"No doubt about it." He grinned. "Now I'm going home and you're going to bed. Alone."

"Myrtle sleeps with me."

"Figures. And Zork?"

"Heavens, no. He stays on the floor at the foot of the bed."

"Then you're pretty safe. There's no room for me in that zoo, anyway. Thank goodness, you just smiled. All is not lost."

"You're a nice person, Mitch Brannon."

"I'm not so sure about that," he said, picking up his jacket and getting to his feet. "Good night, Chelsey Star." He leaned over and kissed her on the forehead.

" 'Night," she said softly.

After he had gone Chelsey pulled her knees up and wrapped her arms around them, resting her chin on top. If she sat there for a month, she thought, she wouldn't be able to sort out the events of the incredible evening. Her behavior with Mitch had been inexcusable. She had acted like a wanton woman, responding shamelessly to his kiss, his touch. She had wanted him. Desire had filled her and she had welcomed it, savored the sensations, held tightly within her embrace the powerful man who had brought her awakening passion to feverish levels. Oh, yes, she had wanted Mitch Brannon to make love to her. It had been with a deep sadness that she had listened to her mind instead of her body and ended the ecstasy.

And her heart? Already it was carrying her further into a world that revolved around Mitch, longing to see him, missing him when he left. He could have become angry with her for calling a halt to their lovemaking tonight. Yet instead he had been patient and understanding, had told her to protect her virtue and wait for the man of her dreams. Oh, no! Could *Mitch* be her Prince Charming? He had brought sunshine to her life, made her glow with an inner happiness, and smile at the mere thought of him.

Chelsey Star was falling in love with Mitch Brannon.

"What a dumb thing to do," she said to a yawning Zork. "Prince Charming is supposed to love me in return. If I keep going on like this, I'll really gum things up."

With a deep sigh, she walked into the bedroom and changed into her nightie. Everyone was present and accounted for. Myrtle was on the foot of the bed, Zork had flopped down on the floor, and Chelsey was snuggled beneath the blankets. But a new entity joined the quiet group. Its name was loneliness.

Dawn found Chelsey consuming a bowl of the vegetable soup for breakfast. During her morning shower she made a firm resolve to spend the day concentrating on computers and not on Mitch Brannon. The thought of falling in love with him was staggering, boggled her mind, and she decided to place the whole subject on mental hold. After packing a sandwich and an orange for her lunch she placed Zork's sunglasses on his eyes, instructed him to collect Myrtle, and put the pair in the backyard.

Upon her arrival at work she was immediately

descended upon by Tony Harrison, who pulled her into a corner.

"Okay, how did you meet the big dude?" Tony asked.

"Who?"

"Mitch Brannon."

"Oh, you know that windshield I broke? Well . . ."

"You're kidding!"

"Nope."

"Why was he at the Crushers' game?"

"He likes baseball."

"Come on, Chels! What's with you and Brannon? Do you know who he is? Hey, that guy is worth big bucks."

"So?"

"Money, Chelsey, lots of it. He lives in the fast lane with—"

"Fast women?"

"All those guys do. Brannon's no different. They have a separate set of rules from us peons. Chels, they walk over people, take what they want, and don't look back. You're getting into a world where you don't belong and you're going to get hurt."

"Tony, Mitch isn't like that."

"Please listen to me! I was at Brannon Development to set up their system. I heard the secretaries talking about gorgeous Mitch and all his women. He changes his ladies faster than his shirts."

"That was five years ago."

"No, Chels. I did an updated expansion last month. One of the women said she didn't know how he worked so hard all day considering how he spent his nights. She didn't mean the guy was playing checkers. He's a womanizer, Chelsey, a rich, spoiled playboy. Lord, he even drives a Ferrari!"

"Tony, I—"

"I care a lot about you, kiddo. Get rid of Brannon, fast. Don't forget, Chels, you're waiting for your Prince Charming. Mitch Brannon does not qualify for the title."

"But—"

"Chelsey," a woman called, "do you have the programs for Barney's Beautiful Bagels?"

"Yes, I'm coming. I'll talk to you later, Tony."

"Remember what I said, Chels."

Tony Harrison was wrong about Mitch, Chelsey thought as she walked to her small, glass-enclosed cubicle. So what if Mitch owned a Ferrari? So did Magnum! Office gossip wasn't worth diddly. Tony was blowing everything out of proportion. Sure Mitch had money and power and could have any woman he wanted, but . . . and, yes, Mitch had kissed her with practiced expertise and a knowing touch, but . . .

"Oh, dammit," Chelsey said.

"Not dammit," someone called back. "It's Barney's Beautiful Bagels!"

By five o'clock Chelsey hated bagels. She was also not overly fond of whoever Barney was for having started the company in the first place. The input of the specialized program into the computers had been tedious, with a multitude of itemized columns. Chelsey had carefully made a backup copy of each disk as it was completed and cross-referenced them into a log.

Once challenging, her job was now drudgery, an endless stretch of hours of punching keys and staring at a small green screen. She often felt guilty that she had used her father's insurance money to pursue a career she now found unrewarding, dull, and boring. If Richard decided he hated accounting, she'd break his nose.

Just before six o'clock, Chelsey walked the last block to her house with weary steps. She was tired, hot, hungry, and had a headache thrown in for good measure. Her eyes widened when she saw Mitch's truck parked in the driveway and she hurried into the yard.

"Hello down there," a voice called.

"Mitch!" She looked up to where he stood on the roof. "What are you doing here?"

"Fixing your roof."

"But you said you had so much work to do at your office."

"I'll explain later. I'll be down in about a half-hour. Oh, there's something in the backyard for you."

"Zork and Myrtle."

"Besides them."

"What is it?"

"Go look. Quit talking to me. I have work to do here. This isn't a roof, it's a sieve."

"It waters my plants when it rains."

"Good-bye, Chelsey."

There was nothing sexy about a man standing on top of a house, Chelsey told herself as she went inside. Well, yes, there was when all he was wearing was tight faded jeans that hung low on his hips and his broad, tanned chest was glistening in the late afternoon sun. Now *that* was sexy.

Chelsey went to the backyard, took one look, and marched right out the front door.

"Mitch!" she yelled. "There's a brand-new ten-speed bike in my yard!"

"I know."

"How did it get there?"

"I bought it for you."

"Why?"

"Because it was my fault yours got stolen."

"No, it wasn't!"

"That's what you said!"

"I was upset at the time."

"But it made sense. If you hadn't waited for me by the car, you wouldn't have had your bike ripped off."

"I'm not keeping it!"

"Yes, you are!"

"I can't accept a gift like that, Mitch."

"It's a payment of a debt, dope."

"No, it's not!"

"Take the bike, Chelsey," Annie yelled out her window. "It's a beauty."

"Thank you, Annie," Mitch hollered.

"You're welcome, Golden Boy!"

"Oh, for Pete's sake," Chelsey said, and stomped into the house. A moment later she was back outside. "Mitch!" she screamed.

"Now what?"

"Since we're going to have a wingding of an argument about the bike that's going to take a while, do you want to stay for dinner?"

"Sure."

"Okay," she said happily, and went back into the house.

Chelsey took a quick shower and pulled on pink shorts and a pink-and-white terry-cloth top before heading for the kitchen.

"Potatoes," she muttered. "He's crazy about potatoes."

She peeled enough potatoes for an army and made a huge tossed salad to accompany the hamburger patties she would fry up when Mitch was finished on the roof. His steady hammering accompanied her as she worked and she continually smiled up at the ceiling.

Tony Harrison was wrong about Mitch, she thought as she set two places at the small table. Playboys didn't spend their time climbing on roofs!

"Done!" Mitch said, coming into the kitchen. "Can I steal a shower? I fried my body up there. I've got some clean clothes in the truck."

"Of course. There's a fresh towel under the sink."

"Thank you, ma'am."

Fifteen minutes later Mitch emerged in khaki shorts and a brown knit shirt. His hair was damp and he smelled like soap when he pulled Chelsey into his arms and kissed her.

"Hello," he said, not releasing his hold.

"Hello," she said, smiling. "Thank you so much for repairing my disaster."

"Don't forget my loaf of bread."

"It's right next to your plate. Come eat."

"In a minute," he said, then kissed her again. "Okay, now we eat."

Chelsey stared at the enormous portions of food on Mitch's plate after he'd served himself and decided she hadn't peeled too many potatoes after all.

"You were going to explain why you were here today," she said.

"My father. He thinks you're the greatest thing since

peanut butter. He's still laughing over that bit in the restaurant about Zork. Anyway, I mentioned I was going to do your roof as soon as we wrapped up this deal we're on, and he threw a fit. The man jumped my butt, said what if it rained in the meantime, and that he and Mike would handle the last details of the thing at the office. So, here I am."

"That was really very nice of him. And you, of course."

"It was just as well because Frank Brannon was about to have an elder son with a broken face. That Mike was on me the minute I walked in about the Great Dane with the sunglasses. I fried his bacon, though."

"What did you do?"

"Pictures, my sweet. I brought my camera over here and took a whole roll of Zork in various stunning poses wearing his glasses. I even got a shot of Myrtle hanging out of his mouth. Michael Mitchell Brannon is going to eat crow."

"Michael Mitchell?"

"Yeah, and I'm Mitchell Michael. You have to understand, Chelsey, I have a very strange set of parents. Want some eight-by-ten glossies of Zork? We could decorate your whole house with them."

"No, thanks. Mitch, you ate that whole loaf of bread!"

"I was hungry. Mind if I polish off those potatoes there?"

"Help yourself while we discuss the bike."

"No can do. I never argue on a full stomach. It's bad for the digestion."

"I can't accept it."

"Indigestion?"

"The bike!"

"Oh, yes, you can."

"No!"

"Chelsey, please," he said seriously. "I really feel badly that you lost the bike your father gave you because you were camped out on the other side of the field waiting for me to show up. I owe you that bike."

"And I have a debt for your windshield. Did you take the Ferrari into the shop?"

"Nope. Didn't have time."

"Tomorrow then?"

"If I have time. I'm very short on time. Just never seem to have enough time. Time is a precious commodity in my life. The last time I had time—"

"Mitch, shut up."

"Right. I think I'll have some more of that salad."

"Help yourself," Chelsey said, laughing softly as he emptied the bowl onto his plate.

"So, tell me, did Harrison come through as expected today?"

"What do you mean?"

"Did he tell you that I'm a rich louse and you should stay away from me?"

"Why do you think Tony would say that, Mitch? Is it true?"

"Yes! No! What I mean is, yeah, I've got bucks, but I already told you that. As far as my personal conduct goes . . . hey, I've never made any phony promises to anyone."

"You're not on trial here, Mitch."

"Did Harrison warn you off or not?"

"Well, yes. Apparently you have quite a reputation around your office as a ladies' man."

"Damn. Chelsey, I have never been out with anyone connected with Brannon Development. It just isn't good policy. I'm not saying I don't enjoy the company of women, but—hell, this isn't going very well. Listen, all I'm trying to say is that I'm not pulling a con on you because I'd never do that. The women I see understand the rules of the game and—"

"Game?"

"Bad word. Chelsey, I think you're wonderful, and you make terrific bread, and kissing you is the high point of my day. Tell Harrison to mind his own damn business! Are you with him all day?"

"No, Tony is the supervisor of the section next to mine."

"Good. Chelsey, we've got something terrific going for us here. Don't let your busybody buddy mess it up."

"Even after last night you feel we have—"

"Yes, dammit, I do! There's more to life than sex. However"—he grinned—"don't ask me to come up with a quick list of ten things."

"Oh, Mitch." Chelsey sighed. "You confuse me so much. I just don't know what you want from me, why you're here. We are so far apart in so many things."

"Nothing that matters. Nothing."

"But—"

"Chelsey, just give us a chance, okay?"

"Okay," she said after a moment. "Would you like a piece of pie?"

"Sure. That will finish off this meal perfectly."

A chance? Chelsey thought as she got up to get Mitch's dessert. To get her heart broken? What was she supposed to do with him? Ship him off to earn a Prince Charming degree?

"Oh, my," she said aloud, laughing. "How silly."

"Your pie is funny?"

"No, I am," she said, handing him the plate containing the huge serving.

"And you're beautiful," he said softly, "and your laughter is the loveliest sound I have ever heard."

Four

Mitch declared that the dishes would have to wait because Chelsey was to test out her new bike before it got dark. Outside on the front sidewalk, Chelsey eyed the candy apple red vehicle skeptically. Zork issued a sharp bark and Mitch said that meant the show was to get on the road.

"I don't know, Mitch," Chelsey said. "It looks awfully complicated."

"Just remember to work the brakes with your hands, not your feet."

"What if I forget? I'll go sailing off the end of the earth!"

"Have you no faith in yourself?"

"You ride it if you're so smart!"

"It's your bike, Chelsey! Put your cute little tush up here."

She smiled. "Do you really think I have a cute tush?"

"Don't change the subject. Up!"

"May my death be on your conscience, Brannon," she

said, climbing on the shiny bike. "Oh-h-h-h," she yelled as Mitch gave the seat a firm shove.

"Come on, Zork," Mitch said as he took off running behind Chelsey. "We're the cheering section."

"Atta girl, Chelsey," Annie called. "See you won the fight, Golden Boy."

"You bet, Annie," Mitch shouted back.

As Chelsey headed down the block with Mitch and Zork in hot pursuit, the occupants of the houses they passed thoroughly enjoyed the spectacle.

"Nice wheels, Chelsey," Polly said. "Hi, Mitch."

"How's life, Polly?" Mitch said. "Still crowded at your place?"

"Ugh."

"Howdy, Chelsey. Howdy, Mitch. Howdy, Zork," Buster said.

"Howdy," Mitch said, waving.

"Ethel, come out here," an old gentleman who was watering his lawn said. "Chelsey has a new toy."

"Shame on you, Chelsey Star!" a woman yelled from a window. "Those contraptions are sinful. The Lord gave us feet to walk on! I'll pray for your soul!"

"Mitch!" Chelsey shrieked. "I'm coming to the corner!"

"Squeeze your hands!"

"Aaak!"

"Both at the same time!"

"Why didn't you say so?"

Chelsey managed to halt her flight and jumped off the bike.

"You did it!" Mitch said, kissing her quickly.

"Pretty good, huh?" She beamed. "It's just a matter of getting the hang of it. Oh, my bottom is numb. That seat is hard. You ride it back to the house."

"Then that lady will have two souls to pray for."

With the bike safely in the backyard and Zork snoozing after the exercise session, Chelsey and Mitch settled on the sofa with glasses of lemonade.

"Thank you, Mitch," Chelsey said. "It's a beautiful

bike. I still feel a little uncomfortable about accepting it, though."

"The discussion is closed. I always pay my debts. The end. Everyone on this street sure knows who you are."

"We sort of look after each other. Most of the people are elderly and we've worked out a signal in case they're ill and need help. They open their drapes first thing in the morning to indicate everything is all right. If they stay closed, we know there's trouble."

"That's nice," he said. "I've never met my neighbors."

"Why not?"

"I don't know. Never had any reason to, I guess. You know, Chelsey, you seem to take on the troubles of the world when in actuality you have enough of your own. Don't you ever get just plain old worn out?"

"Sometimes," she said, nodding, "but things always look better in the morning. My mother used to tell me that. It's a very ancient saying but it works."

"I'll try it sometime."

"Do you live in an apartment, Mitch?"

"No, I have a house, which brings me to my next question."

"Speak."

"Would you like to come over tomorrow night for a swim? I'll barbecue some steaks."

"Sounds like fun."

"Six-thirty? I'll pick you up here."

"Okay."

"No, wait. I'll get you at the bus stop."

"That's not necessary."

"Bus stop."

"Got it."

"I'm going to kiss you a dab, Chelsey. Nothing wild, you understand, but I really do need to kiss you."

"Well, I need to kiss you to thank you for the bike."

"Then we're in complete accord on the subject?"

"Definitely."

Oh, yes, Chelsey thought a second later as Mitch pulled her close and claimed her mouth, there was certainly no argument about that! It was heavenly!

The fluttering kiss intensified as their tongues met and Chelsey's breasts were crushed against Mitch's rock-hard chest. He lifted his head long enough to swing her onto his lap, then again took possession of her mouth. His hand slid under the hem of her shirt to rest on the warm flesh of her back, but he made no attempt to inch around and upward to her breasts, which were aching for his tantalizing touch. She worked her hand under Mitch's shirt, trailing over the curly chest hair, and heard his sharp intake of breath as she found his nipples.

"Chelsey," he growled.

Desire surged through her and she moaned as his mouth devoured hers in a searing kiss. She shifted slightly on his lap, his arousal evident as she moved, and he groaned as his fingertips came to rest just below her full breasts.

"Oh, yes," she whispered. "Please touch me, Mitch."

"No!" he said, taking a shuddering breath. "No more!"

He carefully lifted her off his lap and leaned forward, resting his elbows on his knees and cupping his face in his large hands as he struggled for control.

"Mitch?" Chelsey said, laying her hand on his back, only to have him jerk away.

"Give me a minute," he said, his voice strained.

"I guess I don't know the rules, Mitch," she said softly. "I've never played this game before."

"It's not a game!" He turned to look at her. "It would be a helluva lot easier if it was. I have never in my life desired a woman the way I do you, and I'm not going to do a damn thing about it. I won't make love to you, Chelsey. I just can't."

"You make my virginity sound like a disease!"

"Now that"—he grinned—"was funny."

"No, it wasn't. I'm an unliberated Victorian freak!"

"You, Chelsey Star, are a beautiful, rare, special woman. You are passionate, and giving, and so trusting it scares the hell out of me. You're right, you don't know the rules and so it's up to me to enforce them. I've never been in a situation like this before."

"And you hate it."

"No," he said thoughtfully. "I don't. I'm not crazy about it, but I don't hate it. I'm having to take some responsibility for my actions for a change. It's probably good for my character."

"Mitch, quit joking around!"

"I'm not! The thing is, Chelsey, maybe I'm a real louse and I don't know it."

"Don't be silly."

"It could be true! The women I know operate on a different wavelength."

"I don't want to hear about your crummy women!"

"Oh. Sorry. I was just trying to make a point. There's also the problem of willpower."

"What do you mean?"

"I figure I just have so much allotted to me. I've never tested it before. What if I snap, go berserk, and ravish your body?"

"Oh, for Pete's sake. It takes two to ravish."

"You are seducible, Chelsey."

"I don't think that seducible is a word."

"Sure it is. It means, 'capable of being seduced.' "

"Me? I am?"

"Yep, and that puts me in a helluva bad place. I want you so much I ache inside. We would make beautiful love together, Chelsey. Absolutely beautiful. Dammit, why do you have to trust me so much?"

"Well, excuse me all to hell!"

"Don't swear in front of Zork. He's very impressionable."

"I don't know what you want from me, Mitch!"

"I want you to be just who you are . . . I think. Lord, I'm really confused."

"You? My mind is turning into scrambled eggs!"

"We'll figure this out, Chelsey," he said, pushing himself to his feet. "I'll see you tomorrow night."

"Okay," she said, frowning.

"Hey, don't look so gloomy."

"I don't think all this is supposed to be so complicated."

"Who knows?" He kissed her quickly. "See ya, Zork. 'Bye, Myrtle."

"She can't hear you, remember?"

"It's the thought that counts. *Hasta mañana.*"

As Mitch's truck roared off down the street, Chelsey took the empty glasses into the kitchen and groaned when she saw the forgotten dirty dishes. She ran hot sudsy water in the sink and tackled the chore.

As she washed the dishes she thought about the evening—of how thrilled she'd been to see the shirtless Mitch fixing her roof; how angry and yet secretly pleased she'd been with his gift of the bike; how natural it had been to make him dinner; how much she loved him—

"What?" she yelled, almost dropping a plate and waking up Zork. "I don't! I didn't!" She sighed. "I did. I fell in love with Mitch Brannon."

She sat down at the table to do some serious thinking. Mitch was a wonderful man, a dear, warm, funny, thoughtful person, and it should be no surprise that she'd fallen in love with him. What woman wouldn't? But how many other women believed in Prince Charming, waited twenty-four years for him to show up, knowing that when he did, he'd be the only man she'd ever love?

"What am I going to do, Zork?" He thumped his tail on the floor. "Easy for you to say, but do you think Mitch could ever fall in love with me?"

She stood up and started washing dishes again. Maybe Mitch *would* fall in love with her. Stranger things had happened. In the meantime, she'd just hang in there, enjoy every moment she was with him, enjoy his fantastic kisses—oh, Lord, and that was another problem. Mitch wanted her, but obviously didn't want to want her. Or something like that. He brought her desires swirling to the surface, then said she shouldn't respond to him the way she did. Or maybe he wasn't supposed to respond to her. The whole thing was ridiculous and simply couldn't continue as it was.

She loved Mitch. Falling in love with him wasn't the brightest thing she had ever done, but it was true. It certainly would simplify the situation if he loved her, but he didn't. The rat. So she had to make a decision. Should she make love with the only man she'd ever love even though he didn't love her? If she didn't make love with Mitch, she'd never make love because she couldn't make love with someone she didn't love.

"Did I understand that?" she said aloud. "Yes, I think I did. I'm going to make love with Mitch. I am!"

She nodded with satisfaction, then cleaned the kitchen, swept the floor, and watched an old movie on her small, fuzzy black-and-white television. She slept soundly that night and awoke the next morning feeling, she decided, older, wiser, and very liberated.

The moment Chelsey arrived at work, Tony yanked her into a corner.

"We've got to stop meeting like this," she said.

"Did you get rid of Brannon?"

"No."

"Do it!"

"No."

"Chels, you are making a terrible mistake."

"No."

"Want me to tell you more of the stories I heard about him and his women?"

"No."

"Chelsey!"

"Come by the house sometime, Tony. I'll let you ride my new bike. 'Bye."

"Dammit to hell!" Tony roared.

"No, stupid!" a voice called. "It's Barney's Beautiful Bagels!"

The day was long and dull and a disaster. The electric power dipped just enough to erase the information Chelsey and the others had spent the entire morning typing into the computers. A moan of dismay went up from the entire crew, then with resigned frowns they started over. Everyone in the department took an oath never again to eat bagels.

The grueling hours at last came to an end and there was a smile on Chelsey's face when she stepped off the bus and saw Mitch's truck parked nearby under a shade tree.

"Are you my taxi?" she said, climbing into the cab.

"Yes, ma'am," he said, and leaned over and kissed her.

At the house, Chelsey fed Zork and Myrtle and put them out. She changed into shorts and a blouse and packed her bikini and swim jacket in a tote bag. Just as she and Mitch were about to leave, the telephone rang and she answered it quickly.

"Hi, big sister."

"Richard!" She smiled. "How are you?"

"Sort of fine."

"What does that mean?"

"Chelsey, I broke my ankle."

"What?"

"I slipped on some stairs and, well, it's in a cast and I'm hobbling around on crutches. My boss at the restaurant fired me. That was my fund for supplies, books, all that junk. I went over to the student loan office and—"

"Richard, no! We agreed we wouldn't borrow any money. Don't worry about this. I'll take care of it."

"I can't take any more from you, Chelsey! I'm not even doing my share now."

"Richard, you only have two semesters to go. Please don't give up on me now. Actually this is better because you were exhausted trying to work and study. You take care of that ankle."

"But—"

"Good-bye, sweet brother. I'll write to you soon."

"What's wrong?" Mitch asked as Chelsey slowly hung up the receiver.

"Richard broke his ankle and can't work at the restaurant."

"So now what happens?"

"I'll think of something. Are you ready to go?"

"Chelsey, wait a minute here. Where are you going to get the money?"

"I don't know yet."

"I heard you say you wouldn't borrow any. Why not?"

"If Richard gets a student loan he'll have to pay it back

after he graduates. He's getting married in June and it's just not fair to them to start off with a debt. I walked away with my degree free and clear because of my father's insurance money, and Richard is going to have the same opportunities I had."

"You're not Wonder Woman!"

"I'm not? Well, shucks."

"Chelsey, let me help you. I've got more money than I know what—"

"No! Absolutely not! I already owe you for the windshield. Did you get it fixed?"

"I didn't have time. Look, I'll *loan* you the money if that will make you feel better."

"No, Mitch. Thank you, but I couldn't borrow from you."

"Chelsey, please!"

"I thought we were going swimming."

"You're not being fair to me. It hurts me to know you're in trouble. You're making it worse by not allowing me to help you."

"I'm sorry, Mitch, but I won't change my mind."

"Dammit!"

"Feel better now? Let's go."

Mitch was ominously quiet during the drive across town and had a hard set to his jaw. Chelsey knew he was upset over her refusal to accept his offer of a loan, but she just couldn't borrow from him. She wanted him to be her lover, not her banker! She had bluffed her way through the conversation regarding Richard's news and had kept her voice light and cheerful. In actuality she was petrified! She had to get some money! But where?

Her problems were pushed to the back of her mind when Mitch pulled into a driveway next to a large ranch-style house. The lawn was perfectly manicured and a cobblestone walk led to the front door.

"Oh, Mitch, it's lovely," she said as they entered the enormous living room.

"Like it?"

"I love it."

Her shoes sank into the plush beige carpet as she

wandered slowly around the room. It was done in warm earth tones of brown, tan, orange, and yellow and boasted a good-sized fireplace banked by bookshelves and heavy hand-carved furniture.

"It looks like you," she said.

"I resemble a house?"

"No, the furniture is big and strong, appropriate for your size. It really is a terrific home."

"Thanks. Why don't you get your suit on? You can change in the first bedroom down the hall. I'll meet you by the pool in the back."

"Okay."

The pleasant bedroom had an Indian-design spread on the twin bed and rich dark furniture. It was also bigger than her living room, and the differences between her world and Mitch's came rushing in on her. Everything in Mitch's home was obviously of the finest quality and no expense had been spared. She had never known such luxury, having grown up in a small frame house with a postage-stamp yard. What did Mitch think when he sat on her threadbare sofa? Was it a relief to him to return to this sprawling residence that was as perfect as a picture in a magazine? Was that part of her appeal for him? The chance to see how the other half lived? The novelty of her life?

With a sigh, Chelsey changed into her bikini and covered it with the nonmatching jacket. She passed through a large kitchen on the way to the rear patio where Mitch was lighting the coals on the barbecue. He was wearing blue swimming trunks and she swallowed heavily at the sight of his magnificently proportioned body. Oh, Lord, how she loved him. She longed to rush into his arms and declare him her Prince Charming, tell him of her undying devotion. But Mitch hadn't spoken of love. Their relationship was centering more and more on the growing sexual tension and how it should be resolved. How clinical that sounded.

Well, she had the solution to that little spoke in the wheel. She would come to Mitch freely, offer him what he had called a precious gift, and cherish their union.

What he would not know was that she loved him. Forcing a smile, she walked over to Mitch and placed her hand on his arm.

"Can you really cook?" she asked.

"Sure, I'm great. Chelsey, we have to talk."

"All right, Mitch."

"Come sit down."

Seated on the thickly padded lounge chairs beside the kidney-shaped pool, Mitch stared at his feet for a few minutes as if deeply in thought.

"Chelsey," he said finally, "I can't handle this."

"What's bothering you?"

"The fact that you need money. I have tons of it, and you won't accept my help. I thought we had come further than that. We've shared so much—talked, laughed, been incredibly honest about what we're feeling. Now you're closing a door, leaving me on the outside looking in, and it's ripping me up. Don't do this to us, Chelsey."

"Mitch, I'm trying to forget how wealthy you are because every time I think about it I'm forced to realize how different our worlds and lives are. I blank that from my mind and concentrate on you and how happy I am when I'm with you. If you loaned me money it would ruin everything, force me to continually remember that I'm in your debt when I'd rather be in your arms."

"It wouldn't be like that!"

"Yes, it would. I just can't do it, Mitch."

"And I can't stand helplessly by anymore!"

"Then . . . I guess maybe . . . we shouldn't see each—"

"Don't you say it!" he bellowed. "Don't you even suggest we stop being together or I'll—"

"You'll what?" Chelsey yelled. "Break my kneecaps? Patsy was right. You *are* a hitman!"

"What in the hell am I going to do with you?"

"You could stop hollering for starters. No wonder your neighbors don't drop by. You sound like a raving maniac. I can't help it that I'm broke and you're rolling in money. I will pay for your stupid windshield, but beyond that I suggest that the subject of finances should not come up in our further conversations."

"That's impossible, Chelsey."

"Why? Just zip your lip! Are you going to feed me or not? I'm starving to death."

"Yeah, sure I am, but—don't talk about money at all?".

"No. It's taboo."

"Fine. I'll stew in silence and get an ulcer," he said, raking his hand through his hair.

"Don't you dare! I have enough on my mind without having to worry about your stomach. Oh, damn you, Mitch Brannon. Why can't you like me for myself instead of viewing me as some pathetic little creature with an overdrawn bank account?"

"I—"

"You told me once that women looked at you with dollar signs in their eyes. Well, that's what you're doing to me. You're only seeing what I don't have instead of who I really am. Oh, forget it. I want to go home."

Chelsey got out of the chair and quickly brushed unwanted tears from her cheeks as she stood with her back to Mitch. His strong hands turned her around and pulled her against his chest.

"Oh, Chelsey," he said, holding her tightly. "What have I done? It was so wonderful that you didn't care about my money and now I'm angry because you won't take any of it. I'm sorry, babe. Please try to understand how hard it is for me to know that you're in trouble and I can't help you. And, Chelsey, I do look at you as a woman. A warm, beautiful person. Rich or poor, it doesn't matter. But if you change your mind about the loan—"

"Mitch!"

"No, huh? Damn, you're stubborn."

"I'm also hungry."

"Kiss the cook."

Chelsey kissed the cook.

She kissed him with such intensity that he finally yelled for mercy and detached her hands from what he said was his now broken neck. With arms wrapped around each other they went into the house to make a salad and then emerged to collect the thick steaks Mitch had put on the grill earlier. He produced a bottle of expensive red wine. Chelsey rolled her eyes when he dug a half-dozen foil-wrapped potatoes from beneath the coals on the barbecue.

"Gotta have spuds, my sweet," he said, lathering two at a time with butter once they were seated at a table near the pool. "I realize, of course, that these are not as tasty as Buster's, but we'll make do."

"Everything is delicious," Chelsey said, immensely relieved that the emotionally draining scene regarding her finances was over. Mitch's carefree attitude seemed to have been restored and he made no reference to money throughout the meal.

Chelsey's gaze swept over the beautiful backyard and she felt as though she were at an expensive resort and had just been served the finest on the menu. Mitch accepted this lifestyle so casually, comfortably, and she again registered a sensation of uneasiness. The Brannon family worked hard, had earned the fine things they possessed, but that didn't erase the fact that they had it all. Where did she fit into Mitch's world of riches and glamour? Probably nowhere.

Once the dishes had been stacked in the kitchen they settled on the lounge chairs with one last glass of wine. Mitch had turned the underwater light on in the pool and the crystal-clear water was sparkling and inviting.

"If I swim now I'll sink like a rock," Chelsey said. "I ate like a little piggy."

"I'm glad you enjoyed it. Those stars are winking at me," Mitch said.

"That's because you're so handsome."

"Maybe they're winking at you."

"They twinkle. Stars twinkle, they don't wink."

"Are you sure, Chelsey? I went skinny dipping out here one night and I'm telling you, they winked."

She laughed. "You're so crazy."

"Into the pool, woman," he roared, leaping off the chair and diving into the water in one smooth motion. He surfaced and turned toward Chelsey, treading water as he motioned for her to join him.

She felt suddenly embarrassed, shy, as she stood and removed her jacket. The bikini that had been perfectly adequate when she had put it on now seemed skimpy, barely covering her full breasts and exposing far too much midriff. Mitch's expression did not help one bit as he stared at her with a warm look in his eyes.

"Lovely," he said quietly. "Like a beautiful statue."

Chelsey held her nose and jumped in feet first, spraying water in all directions.

"What form! What grace! What style!" Mitch yelled when she popped back up to the surface.

They swam and floated, had a race, which Chelsey somehow won, and had a marvelous time. Chelsey finally settled on the steps in the shallow end and said she was too exhausted to swim another stroke. Mitch sat down next to her and circled her shoulders with his arm, pulling her close and delivering a very thorough, chlorine-flavored kiss that left her breathless.

"You're all wet," she said, running her hand up his chest.

"As are thou," he said, and claimed her mouth again.

His hands moved over her, warming her cool flesh wherever he touched her. His tongue delved deep within her mouth, finding her tongue and sending shock waves of desire spiraling throughout her body. Suddenly he lifted her in his arms and carried her to a double wide lounge. He laid her down and joined her, holding his body above hers.

"I just want to kiss you, touch you," he said quietly. "I won't hurt you."

Chelsey didn't speak. She simply cupped his rugged, tanned face in her hands and drew him to her, meeting his tongue and drawing lazy circles around it with her own. She could feel his muscles trembling as he held himself in check, and she trailed her fingertips over the moist hair on his hard chest. He gasped as she inched her way to the waistband of his trunks and he moved over her, crushing her with his weight as he devoured her mouth in a searing kiss. Chelsey could feel his arousal pressing against her, relished it, and ached with anticipation of what would come.

For tonight Mitch would be hers. Under the twinkling, winking stars he would consume her with the strength, the power his magnificent body promised. They would become one, and Chelsey would give of herself in total abandonment. There would be no remorse because she loved Mitch Brannon with an intensity that defied description.

"Oh, Chelsey," he moaned. His lips fluttered over her breasts and she pulled loose the tie at the back of her neck, drawing down her top and exposing her throbbing breasts to his smoldering eyes. "Dear heaven," he gasped. "What are you doing? Chelsey, please don't. I—"

She silenced him with a kiss, then his mouth moved to her breasts. He drew one then the other of the rosy nipples into his mouth, bringing each to sweet awareness. Chelsey murmured softly in pleasure and arched her body, pressing closer to Mitch's heated desire.

"No!" he said, his voice strained and harsh as he started to pull away.

"Love me, Mitch," she whispered. "Now. Tonight. I want you so much."

"I can't do this to you!"

"It's my decision. You didn't seduce me until I couldn't think clearly. I want you, all of you. Only you, Mitch. Only you."

"Lord." He took possession of her mouth in a rough, bruising kiss and pressed his hips against hers. Chelsey's desire grew to a raging flame. "But you trusted me," he said, pulling away for a moment. "You trusted me, Chelsey."

"Love me," she whispered. "I *do* trust you. It'll be beautiful just like you said. I've waited so long for you, Mitch."

"Oh, Chelsey, my Chelsey."

She smiled as his hands and lips trailed over her body, then frowned in alarm as she felt Mitch suddenly stiffen. He drew a shuddering breath and pushed himself to his feet, sitting down immediately on another chair and resting his head in his hands.

"Mitch?" she asked anxiously.

"Cover yourself up," he said, his voice choked with emotion.

Chelsey struggled to a sitting position and pulled her top into place, tying it with shaking hands. Tears blurred her vision as the reality of Mitch's rejection struck her like a staggering blow. She stumbled from the chair and put on her jacket, wrapping her arms around herself in a protective gesture.

"Why, Chelsey?" he asked, his voice hushed.

"I wanted you, Mitch," she whispered. "I knew what I was doing."

"So you decided for both of us?" His tone was sharp.

"Well, it's certainly clear to me now that *you* didn't want *me!*"

"Dammit, Chelsey," he said, getting up and grabbing her by the shoulders, "you know how much I want to make love to you!"

"Then why in the hell didn't you?" she yelled, tears spilling over onto her cheeks.

"Maybe you've reached an inner peace about it, but I haven't! You're a virgin, for God's sake! *You* seduced *me!* I almost did something I would have hated myself for. You had no right to do that to me, Chelsey Star! When we make love it will be by mutual agreement."

"What are we going to do? Pencil it in on the calendar? This is insane. I'm the virgin around here, not you. I'm supposed to be the one with the hangups. I was offering myself to you. You! And you refused. I think that really stinks, Mitch Brannon."

"Well, that's just tough. I'm not prepared to take something that belongs to your damn Prince Charming!"

"But you are—"

"And another thing!" he roared. "What if you had gotten pregnant? Did you stop to consider that? Hell, no. You were too busy trying to get into my pants."

"That does it! That really caps it!" She stomped off

toward the house. "Into your pants. The very idea! You've got a gross way of putting things, Brannon."

"What would you call it?"

"Shut up."

In the bedroom, Chelsey changed her clothes in jerky, angry motions, throwing her bikini into the tote bag. Her comb refused to slide through her tangled damp hair and she gave up the attempt. Mitch was standing in the living room when she entered, having put on a T-shirt over his bathing trunks. She brushed by him, out the front door, and climbed into the cab of the truck. Mitch followed her, slamming his door loudly after sliding behind the wheel.

The ride to Chelsey's was completed in record time. Neither spoke and the silence was chilling. When Mitch pulled into the driveway at Chelsey's and stopped, she quickly opened the door.

"I'll see myself in," she said, getting out of the cab.

"Chelsey, wait."

"Good night, Mitch," she said quietly. "Thank you for the dinner."

"Look, I—"

Chelsey hurried to the porch and let herself in the house. Mitch smacked his palm against the steering wheel, then backed out, driving away with a squeal of tires. Inside, Chelsey let Zork and Myrtle in, prepared for bed, and crawled between the sheets. Then, with volume set on high, she burst into tears.

Mitch Brannon was a rotten bum, she thought fiercely. She had never been so humiliated in her life! She had offered him something she had been protecting for twenty-four years and he had rejected her! Just because they hadn't sat down and held a summit conference on whether or not they should make love beneath the damnable winking stars, he didn't want any part of it. What did he plan to do? Have them cast secret ballots? Then he gave her a biology lecture on how babies were made. Well, to be fair, he had a point there. She hadn't thought about that part of it, which was really stupid, but still . . . And what was that noble junk about taking what belonged to her Prince Charming? *He* was the prince, the idiot! Oh, damn, she loved him so much! They had parted in anger and she'd never see him again. He'd probably send a bill collector after her to get the money for his windshield. She hated that Ferrari. She hated potatoes. She hated her roof that didn't leak anymore. But she loved Mitchell Michael Brannon.

After a restless night, Chelsey arrived at work and looked around for Tony so he could drag her into a corner on schedule. When he didn't turn up, she went in search of him and offered to buy him a cup of coffee.

"Sure, Chels," he said. "What's up?"

"Tony, is your section still involved in that big project for the lumberyard?"

"Yep. It's a killer. Every nail, board, you name it, is going on inventory disks."

"And there's overtime work available?"

"Yes."

"I need those extra hours, Tony."

"Why?"

"Richard broke his ankle and lost his job."

"Whew. Rough. Okay, report at closing time. I'll set you up. Are you sure you can handle it? I hate to see you do this."

"I have no choice. I'll see you later."

"By the way," Tony said, "how's Brannon?"

" 'Bye, Tony."

Chelsey called Polly at work and asked if she'd go to the house that evening and feed Zork and Myrtle. The spare key was under the mat on the back porch and the pet food was kept in the kitchen. Polly agreed but expressed concern over Chelsey's decision to take on the extra workload.

"It'll be a snap," Chelsey said cheerfully, then rolled her eyes in dismay as she hung up the receiver.

When she let herself into the house that night at ten o'clock she was numb. Her head ached and every time she shut her eyes she saw little numbers dancing across a green computer screen. She mumbled a hello to her pets, fell sideways across her double bed, and slept. The next day was a repeat performance and it was again nearly ten before she arrived home.

Tony had hovered around at work like a concerned father and continually told Chelsey she couldn't keep up the pace. She assured him she was doing absolutely fine, causing him to throw up his hands in defeat and storm off down the hall.

On Friday morning, Chelsey was so exhausted she could hardly drag herself out of bed and her reflection in the mirror showed dark circles under her eyes.

It was amazing, she decided as she headed for her cubicle at work, how she had found the time and mental energy to miss Mitch, to ache for his touch and kiss, and yearn to hear his laughter. His image had crept up on her when she least expected it, often causing sudden tears to spring to her eyes. She remembered with crystal clarity his angry words when he had accused *her* of seducing *him* and how he had declared her actions to have been unfair.

She simply didn't understand his attitude. If she was willing to give herself to him, why hadn't he just taken what she offered and had a wonderful time? That's how men did that sort of stuff, right? She had asked nothing in return, no commitment or declaration of love in exchange for her virtue. So what was his problem, for Pete's sake? She'd never know because he wouldn't be around to explain it to her. Mitch was gone.

Chelsey had always refused to see again men who tried to pressure her into bed, but it seemed incredible that she had been dumped by a man who refused to accept her willingness to do just that! It was confusing, infuriating . . . and sad. They just weren't making Prince Charmings the way they had in Cinderella's day. The modern specimens were definitely strange.

As Chelsey walked the last block to her house at ten-fifteen on Friday night she had to concentrate on placing one foot in front of the other. Her body was not performing correctly and there was a loud rushing noise in her ears. She ached from head to toe and felt sluggish and heavy. If she could only keep her feet moving she could get home to bed and sleep the weekend away.

Suddenly she smacked into something hard and gasped in surprise. Mitch's truck was parked in the driveway! The door to the cab flew open and in a moment she was being tightly gripped by the shoulders.

"Where in the hell have you been?" Mitch roared. "I've been looking for you every night since— What's wrong with you?"

"Huh?"

"Chelsey, talk to me! Are you all right?"

She opened her mouth to speak but nothing came out. She simply stared up at Mitch as if she'd never seen him before in her life, then everything went black.

Five

"Chelsey? Please, babe, wake up!"

Whoever the pest was, she wished he'd go away, Chelsey thought foggily. No, now wait a minute. The pest was . . . "Mitch!" she whispered, opening her eyes.

"Oh, thank God! I thought you were dying or something."

"What happened?"

"You fainted right into my arms. That stuff looks great in the movies, but you scared the hell out of me. I brought you in here to your bed."

"Where's Zork and Myrtle?"

"I don't know. Outside, I guess."

"Oh, those poor things! I've—"

"Don't you move!" Mitch said, getting quickly to his feet. "I'll go let them in. Don't even blink."

With Zork and Myrtle in attendance, Mitch sat back down on the edge of the bed and held Chelsey's hand in his.

"What's going on?" he asked softly. "Where have you been every night?"

"Working at the office."

"Damn," he said, taking a deep breath and looking at the ceiling for a moment before redirecting his frowning gaze at her. "I was afraid of that. You look terrible."

"You look beautiful." She smiled, relishing the sight of him in tight faded jeans and a deep blue western shirt.

"I've been out of my mind with worry. I came by every night and when I saw you weren't home, I assumed you were out with Tony or someone."

"Why didn't you just call me at work?"

"Because—because I wanted to *see* you, not try to talk things out on the phone when you were at work and might hang up on me. Oh, Chelsey, how could you do this to yourself, to me, to us? Didn't you give one thought to what I might be going through when I couldn't find you? And now to see you so worn out . . . Hey, I know we had a bit of a misunderstanding the last time we were together, but—"

"Did you get the windshield fixed?"

"I didn't have time. Chelsey, you're not doing this anymore! No more, do you hear me? You tell them you're finished with the overtime bit. Are you listening to me?"

"The whole neighborhood heard you! Oh, my head."

"It hurts? Lord, I'm sorry. Are you hungry? I'll fix you something to eat."

"No, I really don't want anything. Mitch, why are you here?"

"Why am I here? You can ask me why I'm here?"

"The question did come to the front of my mind, yes."

"Because I couldn't find you! Because I haven't slept since that night you were at my house! Because you're driving me crazy! That's why I'm here!"

"Oh."

"Go to sleep."

"You sit there screaming your head off at me and then calmly tell me to go to sleep?" She attempted to sit up, only to have Mitch push her back against the pillow.

"Yeah, go to sleep! You look like death warmed over.

You're going to rest if I have to sit on you! And then, and then, Chelsey Star, we are going to have a lengthy discussion regarding your behavior."

"Oh, is that so!"

"Take your clothes off."

"What?"

"You'll sleep better in your pajamas or nightgown or your Dr. Denton's."

"Dr. Denton's? Oh, you're cute, Mitch. Just too cute for words." She folded her arms over her breasts. "Go home."

"Nope," he said, tugging off his shoes.

"And what, pray tell, do you think you're doing?"

"Here it is, short and sweet. You apparently don't have enough brains in your pretty head to know that you're exhausted and have pushed yourself too far this time. You are staying in that bed until I say you can get out. You may go to the bathroom if you raise your hand and ask permission to leave the room. If you attempt to cross me on this, I'm going to turn you over my knee and whop you! In the meantime, I'm not letting you out of my sight. Any questions?"

"You're spending the night here?"

"Yep."

"That's the dumbest thing I've ever heard." Chelsey frowned. "I'm a little old for a babysitter."

"Woman, you need a keeper! Damn, I'd better go hide my truck around the corner. Your neighborhood fan club will have a field day with this."

"Leave it," she said, waving her hand breezily in the air. "Annie will be thrilled."

"Go to sleep."

"Would you quit saying that?"

"Where's your nightgown or whatever?"

"Under my pillow."

"Why?"

"Because that's where I keep it!"

"You're weird." He tugged the sheer, short nightie out from beneath her head. "Say now, this is interesting. Nice little see-through number here."

"Give me that!" she said, snatching it out of his hands.

"Five minutes max. I'll be back." He got up and strode from the room.

Chelsey scrambled out of the bed, tore off her clothes, and after donning the nightie over her bikini panties dove back under the blankets. There was no doubt whatsoever in her mind that Mitch meant every word of what he said. The man was a lunatic! The man was also the most wonderful sight she could have possibly wished to see, and she was smiling when he came stalking back into the room.

"Very good," he said, sitting down on the edge of the bed. "I see you understand how this is going to go."

"Mitch, it really isn't necessary for you to stay and—"

"Chelsey, you have put me through a living hell the past few days. From now on, I'm running the show!"

"Oh, Mitch," she said, placing her hand on his cheek. "I'm sorry if—"

"Oh, no, you don't." He jumped to his feet. "Keep your paws off me, lady!"

"Huh?"

"You're not going to seduce me, Chelsey Star."

"What?" she said, bursting into laughter.

"I have my principles." He thumped himself on the chest.

"Mitch, are we playing role reversal? I think those are my lines."

"Go . . . to . . . sleep!" he growled, storming out the door.

"My goodness," Chelsey said as she turned out the light. "He certainly is upset."

"Damn it to hell!" Mitch roared, coming back into the room and nearly falling over a snoring Zork.

"Now what's wrong?"

"I can't sleep on that sofa! It's lumpy and my feet hang over the end. You'll have to share, but keep your hands to yourself!"

"I wouldn't dream of touching your virtuous body,

Brannon." She flopped over onto her stomach, smothering her giggle in the pillow.

Chelsey felt the mattress give under Mitch's weight and peered at him with one eye. The moon and the twinkling, winking stars had cast a silvery luminescence over the room. Mitch's massive frame was outlined in the almost eerie light and her heart raced at the sight of his bare chest and the snug jeans that rode low on his narrow hips. He had his arms crossed under his head and seemed to be staring up at the ceiling. Chelsey longed to reach out and tangle her fingers in the curly mass of hair on his chest, lie close to his side and feel the heat and strength emanating from his body.

But, she decided, if she made one move in his direction he'd probably break her nose! Mitch had made it very clear that he had been extremely concerned when he couldn't find her the past few days and was now worried because she was thoroughly exhausted. But why? What emotion was prompting his rantings and ravings? Was he viewing her as a protective older brother might a younger sister? How awful! Was it pity? Insulting! She loved him so much, but what did he feel for her? He—

Mitch sneezed.

"Myrtle!" Chelsey said, sitting bolt upright on the bed. "I forgot!"

She jumped off the bed, grabbed Myrtle, and took her into the living room. When she returned to the bedroom she closed the door to keep the cat safely away from Mitch. She was unaware that her figure was clearly outlined beneath the sheer material of the nightie as she crawled onto the bed and leaned over Mitch.

"Are you all right?" she asked. "I should never have let her in here."

"Oh, God, Chelsey, please!" Mitch moaned.

"Myrtle made you sick?"

He grabbed her by the shoulders and flung her over onto her back, covering her body with his as she stared up at him in wide-eyed shock.

"You are parading around half naked," he growled close to her lips.

"You told me to put my nightie on!"

"Oh, damn," he whispered, and claimed her mouth in a long kiss that thoroughly revitalized Chelsey's exhausted body. "Don't ever, *ever* disappear on me again," he said huskily, his face only inches from hers. "I want to know where you are and what you're doing. Got it?"

"Well, I—"

"Chelsey!"

"Got it!"

"I am now removing my person from on top of your person and no further words will be spoken in this room until tomorrow," he said through clenched teeth, then rolled away and flung his arm over his eyes.

"Whew!" Chelsey said, checking her heart to see if it was returning to a reasonable pace. She was so acutely aware of Mitch's presence next to her she thought she would jump out of her skin. That kiss had been ecstasy, but she needed about a dozen more to erase the loneliness of the past days. The entire situation was asinine! She was in bed with the man she loved—and they were having a slumber party! Maybe if she just wiggled over there and . . . no, Mitch was not behaving like Mr. Sunshine. She'd better mind her manners. And she was so very, very tired. Tomorrow they'd talk and straighten everything out. Tomorrow.

Chelsey stirred and opened her eyes, then caught her breath in shock. She was curled up closely to Mitch's body and one of his arms was resting under her breasts. Sunlight filled the room and Zork's snoring broke the peaceful silence.

How had she gotten over to Mitch's side of the bed? Had she reached for him in her sleep, or had he scooped her up and brought her there? Whichever was the case, she was held fast by the heavy weight of his arm. His steady breathing indicated he was deeply asleep and she lifted her head slightly to glance at his beard-roughened face.

Oh, how sweet, she thought. Except for that beard, he looked like a little boy with his blond hair all tousled and his features relaxed. How gentle he appeared when he wasn't hollering, which was his favorite pastime lately. He certainly had a healthy pair of lungs. That wasn't all that was in excellent shape in regard to Mr. Brannon, and Chelsey closed her eyes in contentment as she rested her head on his hard chest and fell back to sleep.

When she awoke again it was nearly ten o'clock and she was alone in the bed except for Myrtle and a note on Mitch's pillow which read, "Zork and I had some errands to run. Do not move! Mitch."

"Bossy man," she said, shuffling into the bathroom to take a shower.

She had just dressed in shorts and a top and walked into the living room when she heard Mitch's truck in the driveway. On impulse, she ran back into the bedroom and jumped into bed, pulling the blankets up to her chin.

There was no sense in getting Mitch all in a dither first thing in the morning, she decided. If he started yelling again the plaster was going to crack in her poor little house.

"Hi, Zork," she said as the Great Dane padded into the bedroom. "Hey, look at those snazzy glasses!"

"Candy apple red to match your bike," Mitch said, following close behind. "You'll be the dynamic duo when you go riding. I'm glad to see you're still in bed."

"That's where I am all right, but I feel very rested."

"You look better. You may get up, Miss Star, and I will fix you some breakfast. Come on, Zork, we have to unload the truck."

"Thank you, mighty master," she mumbled as the pair left the room.

"I heard that!" Mitch called.

Chelsey made the bed, banged a few dresser drawers, and ran water in the bathroom sink. When she had used up what she hoped was the appropriate amount of time, she headed for the kitchen.

"Good heavens," she said, "what is all this?"

"Food, my sweet," Mitch said as he stirred something on the stove.

"There's enough for an army!" Chelsey said, her gaze sweeping over the supplies that were set in every available spot. "How much do I owe you for—oops," she said, as Mitch gave her a stormy glare.

"Sit," he said. "No, wait." He walked over to her and kissed her deeply. "Now you sit."

Chelsey sank onto a chair at the small table and peered at the array of canned goods. There was everything imaginable and all were the most expensive brands. She would not accept this food from Mitch. She felt like a charity case where little old ladies with mink stoles and blue hair came to the door and presented needy souls with baskets of groceries. There was even a can of artichoke hearts, for Pete's sake!

"Mitch, about all this stuff. I—"

"Eat up," he said. He set a plate of scrambled eggs and sausage in front of her and joined her with a huge serving of his own. "The food is for me. I have a very big appetite and since I'm spending the weekend here—"

"You're what?"

"I told you, I'm not letting you out of my sight."

"But—"

"Annie Oakley to OK Corral," the box squawked.

"I'll get it," Mitch said, going into the living room. "Hi, Annie, how's life?"

" 'Morning, Golden Boy. Everything okay over there?"

"Under control, Annie."

"Glad you're on the scene, Golden Boy. Over and out."

"See ya, Annie."

Chelsey opened her mouth to speak as Mitch sat back down opposite her. Then she changed her mind, sighed, and directed her attention to the breakfast. It tasted delicious and she polished it off in short order. She only then realized that Mitch was clean-shaven and dressed in a blue T-shirt and cutoff jeans instead of his clothes of the night before. He and Zork must have stopped by his house in their morning travels.

"You go in the living room," Mitch said when he was finished. "I'll clean up here."

"Mitch, I can wash my own dishes!"

"Don't argue, Chelsey."

"Damn," she said, tilting her nose in the air and marching out of the kitchen.

She sat on the sofa with her arms folded over her breasts and a scowl on her face while Mitch banged away in the kitchen. Zork had apparently decided to stay with his buddy and she could hear Mitch chatting with the dog. Zork, she fumed, had sold out for a pair of candy apple red sunglasses!

"All right," Mitch said when he came into the room and sat on the sofa. "We talk."

"About what?"

"You. Me. Us. Everything."

"That's a lot of topics."

"Quit pouting, Chelsey."

"Well, you're being a bully!"

"Just listen, okay?" he said firmly. "When two people enter into a relationship, which is what I like to believe we have done, they have certain responsibilities for the other person."

"Such as?" Relationship? she thought. My, what a nice word.

"Making sure they do not cause that individual any undue mental anxiety by the way they conduct themselves. They don't flirt or—"

"Who flirted?" Chelsey yelled.

"No one! That was an example!"

"Oh."

"You, Chelsey Star, have not been kind to me. You disappeared into thin air, refused to accept my financial assistance, upset my sleep pattern, affected my ability to work, and got my mother mad at me."

"Your mother? What does she have to do with this?"

"She invited us over for dinner and I had to tell her I couldn't find you at the moment. She said I'd lose my head if it wasn't attached, and how could I have lost track of such a darling girl. In short, you've made my life hell and it's going to stop!"

"Mitch, I—"

"This," he said, yanking some papers out of his back pocket, "is a check for three thousand dollars and a promissory note saying you will pay it back to me in fifty-dollar monthly installments starting next June."

"No!"

"Yes! We are compromising, which is also part of relationships. I want to give you this money but will settle for loaning it to you. I can't take it anymore, Chelsey. It's killing me to see you working so hard and worrying about Richard's expenses. We've got to remove it from our world together."

"Remove it?" she said, fighting back her tears. "You're putting money between us, Mitch. You're the banker and I'm the bankee. Is that a word? Never mind. The point is, business dealings have no place in the lives of people who are—are whatever we are. I won't say lovers because the title doesn't fit."

"Chelsey, babe, please. If I know you're financially secure I'll be able to relax and enjoy being with you like when we first met. Sign the note. Do this for me, us, then we can forget about it and get on with . . . other things."

"It isn't going to work that way!"

"Trust me," he said, picking up a pen and placing it in her hand.

Chelsey looked at Mitch's face, saw the concern and the worry lines across his forehead. It was wrong, terribly wrong. The loan would bring an element into their lives that had no place being there. She would feel she would have to justify every penny she spent to assure Mitch she had used the funds in the manner in which he had intended. She would be in his debt instead of his arms, and it would destroy them. But he was convinced that the assurance of her financial well-being would restore him to his carefree frame of mind and there was no changing his beliefs.

"I'll sign the note," she said softly. "I appreciate your generosity."

"Thank God," he said, letting out a breath of relief as she scribbled her name on the paper.

"What about the windshield for the Ferrari?"

"We'll settle up on that when I have time to get it fixed."

"Is this conference concluded?" she asked.

"Not quite. We have to discuss what happened at my house."

"I'd rather not, Mitch."

"It's important, Chelsey. You made a momentous decision that night."

"I'm aware of that! I also remember being thoroughly rejected and sent to my room!"

"I did not reject you!"

"What would you call it?"

"I . . . I used restraint."

"And what gave you that right, Mitch? My body belongs to me and what I do with it is my business. If I want to experience lovemaking with the most wonderful man I have ever known then I will. I won't have you treating me like a child who doesn't know her own mind. I am a woman! If you don't want me, then—then I'll find someone who does."

"Like hell you will!"

"Oh, be quiet. I didn't mean that and you know it."

"You could have gotten pregnant."

"Which would have been my problem, not yours. I'm not asking anything of you, Mitchell Brannon. I'm so sick of talking about this sex thing. It's definitely losing its appeal. I think I'll become a nun and live with Polly."

"You're driving me crazy again!" he said, raking his hand through his hair. "I'm trying to do what's best for you."

"What makes you think you know what that is?"

"Well, I—I don't know. I just didn't want you to rush into something you'd regret later."

"Really? Or is it the other way around, Mitch? Are you afraid you'd feel so guilty you'd have a sense of responsibility you want no part of? You're used to worldly women who pop birth control pills like vitamins. Heaven forbid you should mess up the psyche of an innocent little virgin who fell under your seductive charm. You've got an overblown ego. I'm not going to pine away for you for the rest of my life just because you were the first man to make love to me."

"You're not?"

"No!"

"What do you plan to do? Use my body and throw me out?"

"Oh, for Pete's sake!" Chelsey yelled. "I refuse to discuss this any further. It's totally ridiculous. You talk about compromise but only when it suits your needs. What I want isn't important."

"There is no half way about making love, Chelsey. You either do it or you don't."

"Well, I was going to 'do' but now I 'don't' believe I will."

"Why not?"

"Because we're talking it to death. People don't spend this much time deciding what car to buy. There is definitely something wrong with our relationship, Mitch."

"Don't say that, Chelsey."

"It's true," she said, her voice low. "We're all caught up in arguments about money and lifestyles and sex. It's not supposed to be this way. We should just know what's right and good and what would make each other happy. We're working too hard at this and gumming it all up."

"Really?"

"Really."

"You may have a point there." Mitch nodded thoughtfully. "Maybe we should pull back and regroup."

"Meaning?"

"The money thing is taken care of and needn't come up again. Your working overtime is also out of the way. The roof is fixed so you're no longer living in a leaky house and you have a new bike. Actually, we've accomplished a great deal. As I see it, we're in pretty good shape here."

Chelsey frowned. "Forgot something, didn't you?"

"The sex number? No, I haven't forgotten it at all. I owe you an apology on that one."

"You do?"

"Yep." He laced his fingers behind his head and leaned back. "I do. I now realize you are an adult woman who controls her own destiny."

"I am?"

"Absolutely. My concerns were misguided and uncalled for."

"They were?"

"Goodness, yes. After all, it is your body we're talking about here. Mine isn't that important because it's been down that road since I was fifteen years old."

"It has? Fifteen? Good Lord, that's terrible."

"I was a fast-maturing kid. Anyway, the point here is, whatever you decide to do is fine with me. If you want to make love, we'll just jump right in and get the job done."

"That's gross."

"Hey, you want to be in command of yourself in that area and I thoroughly agree you have every right to do that. Just let me know if you want me to take my clothes off."

"Mitch, for heaven's sake!"

"Yes?" he said, an expression of pure innocence on his face.

"I—nothing. All right, fine. Then we are in complete agreement."

"We certainly are." He nodded. "Oh, who's in charge of birth control? Maybe we should settle that just in case you decide to . . . you know."

"Well—um . . ."

"I'll take care of it," he said, patting her knee.

"I suppose you've been doing that bit since you were fifteen too."

"Sure." He smiled smugly. "Well, we've covered everything on the agenda. Come on, I'll buy you and Zork an ice cream cone. Then I think you should take a nap. I don't want you to overdo it."

"I'm not tired."

"We'll see." He walked over to the box on the wall and

pushed the button. "Hey, Annie," he said, "want us to bring you back some ice cream?"

"You betcha, Golden Boy. Chocolate. Two scoops."

"You're on."

"Thanks, sweetheart," Annie said. "Over and out."

"She's a cool lady," Mitch said. "I've never met her, but I like her. What are you frowning about, Chelsey? Don't you want ice cream?"

"Huh? Oh, yes, of course I do."

"Let's go. Where's Zork's sunglasses?"

Mitch seemed oblivious to the fact that Chelsey was very quiet during the outing to the ice-cream stand and the stroll through the park while they licked their treats. Zork thoroughly enjoyed his triple-decker chocolate chip with a sugar cone, but Chelsey hardly tasted hers.

She found herself glancing often at Mitch, waiting for him to tell her that the sexual liberation he had handed her on a silver platter was all a joke. Any minute now he would say that he had been kidding, that he had no intention of accepting her precious gift unless they had thoroughly discussed it and agreed that the time was right for both of them.

When Mitch said they should head back and purchase Annie's ice cream and have it put in a cup so it wouldn't melt, Chelsey realized the subject of sex was closed. Mitch had meant it! He was simply going to wait for a signal from her and then start tearing off his clothes!

Well, that was what she wanted, right? She had demanded the control of her own body and won the battle. So why did it all seem so cold and unfeeling? Talk about casual sex! Mitch was now so laid back on the topic of Chelsey's virginity he was practically falling asleep with boredom. They either would or wouldn't, so what was the big deal, was the impression the bum was giving. Didn't he realize how important this was to her? Well, what did she expect from a man who had been doing that stuff since he was fifteen years old? It was a wonder he hadn't worn out his equipment!

Somehow Mitch's about-face was . . . well, unsettling. And Chelsey was becoming increasingly muddled by her own reactions. She had been so sure of her intentions that night at his house, hurt and angered by his rejection, and now felt almost betrayed that he was taking the whole situation so lightly.

Darn it, what was wrong with her? She was in love with this man, needed, wanted to belong to him in every sense of the word. She was now free to give of herself and receive from him in return. So why wasn't she happy that the matter had been resolved and things could follow their natural course? It was, without a doubt, very confusing.

Back at the house, Chelsey delivered Annie's ice cream and received a knowing wink from the feisty old woman.

"Nap time," Mitch said when Chelsey reentered the living room.

"Yes, I think you're right," she said. "I'm a little tired."

"Sleep well, babe," he said, pulling her close and kissing her. "I'm going to toss a ball to Zork for a while."

"You two certainly have become fast friends."

"He's a great horse."

In spite of the turmoil in her mind, Chelsey dozed off almost immediately after stretching out on the bed. Myrtle curled up next to her and she mumbled an apology to the cat for having banned her from the bedroom the previous night. When Chelsey awoke an hour later she once again found a note from Mitch stating that he and Zork had gone for a ride with the new bike.

Chelsey brushed her hair until it glowed with auburn highlights, then wandered into her well-stocked kitchen. She ate two oranges, a banana, and a huge bunch of grapes before flopping onto the sofa with a frown on her face. Her gaze swept over the meager furnishings, seeing them as they must appear to Mitch. Grim. Her entire house could fit into his living room. Everything was so shabby and even the plants were drooping. Had her beautiful hardwood floors always been so scratched? Mitch had complained that the sofa was lumpy and—

"We have returned!" he suddenly exclaimed, striding in the front door with Zork close on his heels.

"Have fun?" Chelsey asked.

"Great bike. Oh, greetings from everyone on the block and my soul is being prayed for again," he added as he removed Zork's candy apple red sunglasses.

"Mitch, do you think this room is sort of . . . blah?"

"Blah?"

"Drab, bare, yucky."

"Well, it's . . . unique, cute. It could use a bit more furniture. I mean, the plants are nice, but . . ."

"Yeah, I know."

"Hey, we could go shopping tomorrow for new stuff for in here. That would be fun."

"I couldn't afford it."

"Sure you could. You just got a good-sized check, remember? Richard doesn't need all of it and the rest is yours for whatever you want."

"But that's your money."

"It absolutely is not. You're paying it all back starting next summer. Why not shape the place up in the meantime?"

"I'm not sure I'd feel right about spending any of it on—on . . ."

"Why not? There's no condition attached to it. Set aside what you need for Richard's expenses, and then enjoy."

"Well, maybe just another chair."

"That sofa is a disaster, Chelsey. The spring on the end cushion is going to pop through at any minute."

"Really?"

"I tried sleeping on that thing, remember?"

"Maybe we could just go browse," she said. "It would be a nice outing."

"Okay. Want some lunch?"

"I had some fruit."

"Come talk to me while I eat, then. Did you sleep?"

Chelsey laughed. "Yes, I was a good girl."

"Well, in that case, I'll take you to the movies tonight."

"You're ever so kind."

"I know, I'm terrific," he said, pulling her into his arms. "Kiss me, you gorgeous creature."

The kiss was so nice. It was gentle and lingering and sensuously soft. Chelsey leaned into the hard contours of Mitch's body and relished the feel of his strong arms holding her tightly against him. He smelled deliciously like aftershave and male perspiration from his bike ride, and she could feel desire beginning to stir.

"Food," Mitch said, close to her lips. "I'm going to pass out from hunger."

"Heaven forbid. On to the kitchen."

Mitch concocted a huge sandwich, added a pile of fruit to his plate, and consumed it all with a quart of milk.

"I can't buy furniture!" Chelsey said suddenly. "I forgot about the Ferrari."

"We'll work that out on a separate plan," Mitch said, picking up another bunch of grapes. "It probably won't cost that much anyway."

"When are you going to have it fixed? Yeah, I know, when you have time."

"Yep. Don't cop out on our shopping trip. I'm really looking forward to it. How about a sexy furry sofa?"

"No!"

"Satin and leather?"

"Mitch, that's kinky!"

"Just making suggestions."

"Eat your grapes."

They spent the remainder of the afternoon watching a baseball game on the fuzzy television set and Mitch scolded Zork, telling the dog he was rooting for the wrong team. Dinner was pork chops, a great pile of potatoes, and an enormous fruit salad. Mitch brought in clean clothes from the truck and informed Chelsey that since he was such a gentleman she could have the shower first.

"Just don't use all the hot water," he said.

"You're getting pushy again, Brannon."

"Well, if you sentence me to a cold shower I'll figure you're trying to tell me something." He grinned. "It will be construed as subtle communication."

"Not really," she said. "I happen to have a very small

water heater and since we already washed all those dishes I doubt if there's any hot stuff left."

"Then I shouldn't read a message into the condition of my shower?"

"Nope."

"Whatever you say, my sweet."

The water was indeed ice cold and Chelsey was in and out of the shower in record time. She was frowning slightly as she dressed in white slacks and a kelly green blouse that accentuated the rich color of her hair. Mitch was making no bones about the fact that he had delegated full responsibility for their sexual activity, or lack of it, to her. He appeared unconcerned as to how it would go and was calmly waiting for her to tell him. How could such a virile man suddenly become so blasé about the whole thing? Sure he had self-control and willpower, but it was getting ridiculous! Didn't he want to make love with her? Of course he did! That was evident every time he kissed her.

This whole situation didn't seem right somehow. Their lovemaking should be a mutually agreed upon step forward in their relationship, not one person pushing the other's buttons! She had waged a war and won the right of control, and now she didn't want it! Lord, she had a big mouth. She'd gotten herself into this mess and had absolutely no idea what to do.

"Oh, for Pete's sake," she said, stomping into the living room.

"What's wrong?"

"Huh? Nothing. Cold showers make me crabby."

"Oh. I'll be ready in a flash and we'll go. You sure look pretty, Chelsey. Your hair is the color of an Irish setter's."

She laughed. "Thanks a bunch!"

"That's a compliment! Irish setters are gorgeous. Oh, hi, Zork, old pal. Setters don't compare to Great Danes. No contest. You're top-notch, buddy."

Chelsey shook her head as the pair disappeared into the bedroom, Mitch delivering a nonstop dissertation to Zork on the dog's attributes and especially handsome profile. Mitch was so funny and Chelsey's love for him seemed to grow stronger every minute. It felt so natural, so comfortable to have him in her shower, kitchen, living room. And bed? There was that question again. The one that was turning her brain into mush.

One thing was certain, though. When the weekend was over she would miss Mitch's presence, the sight, the aroma, the feel of him. Her little house would seem terribly empty and quiet without his massive form and throaty laughter. If only he loved her in return. They could spend a lifetime together until death parted them. He truly cared for her, she knew he did, but he had never said he loved her. Her Prince Charming had a flaw. He had forgotten to fall in love with the princess.

Mitch emerged from the bedroom in dark slacks and an open-neck yellow shirt and instructed Zork to pick up Myrtle and haul her out to the backyard. Chelsey called Annie on the box to make sure the older woman was all right and was informed that Chelsey should be concentrating on that Golden Boy instead of talking to the neighbors.

"Good night, Annie," Chelsey said, rolling her eyes.

"We should get Annie a boyfriend," Mitch said. "Polly too. Everyone should have someone."

"Oh?"

"I, for one, used to think that variety was the spice of life. But now I can see the advantages to feeling comfortable in one individual's presence."

"Do tell," Chelsey said, smiling.

"Absolutely. It saves a great deal of time, fuss, and bother."

"About what?"

"Potatoes, of course. You just don't know what a relief it is to know I can count on you to make me potatoes. It's a heavy load off my mental anguish."

"You're bonkers, Brannon."

"It runs in my family. Ready to go?"

As they drove away from the house in Mitch's truck, he picked up Chelsey's hand and kissed the palm. "You look so much better now," he said. "You sure scared me last night."

"I'm fine. I was only tired and I've certainly slept enough to make up for it."

"Well, as long as I know you're back on your feet, I'll go on home tonight."

"But you said . . ."

"I know, but at the time I forgot I had plans."

"Plans?"

"Yeah, I've got a date first thing in the morning."

Six

"You've got a what?" Chelsey shrieked.

"A golf date with Mike. We play really early before it gets too hot."

"Oh," she said, bursting into laughter.

"That's funny?"

"No, sorry."

"Anyway, there's no sense in me banging around waking you up. I'll get you after lunch and we'll go looking at furniture. I hope this movie isn't too crowded. I hate long lines."

Mitch was going home? she wondered wildly. He was supposed to spend another night and then if she decided to . . . you know, all she'd have to do was slither over to his side of the bed. But now he wouldn't even be there! Maybe that was just as well since she did need some time to adjust to her newfound liberation. Of course, he still had to take her back to the house after the movie. But if they made love he'd leave later and that sneaking off in the middle of the night stuff was tacky.

But then again—oh, forget it. She was going to think herself to death at this rate.

The movie was a spy thriller that had the bad guys leaping out of dark corners and Chelsey continually grabbed Mitch's arm in a viselike grip.

"I'm going to be black and blue for life," he whispered, prying her fingers loose.

"Sorry, it's just so—oh, Lord!" she yelled, as a villain attacked the handsome hero.

"Would you keep it down, lady?" a man said.

"She really gets into these things, buddy," Mitch said cheerfully.

"It sounds like you're killing her over there," the man replied.

"Clam up, you people!" a woman bellowed.

"Says who?" the man shouted.

"Oh, for heaven's sake," Chelsey said, "everybody be quiet!"

"You started it," Mitch whispered.

"Shh," four people said at once.

"Aaak!" Chelsey screamed as the fearless hero was knocked off the end of a pier and descended upon by a slimy alligator.

"That's it!" Mitch roared, hauling her out of her seat and up the aisle. "You broke my arm! You broke my lousy arm!"

"I didn't mean to!" Chelsey yelled.

"Take her to see *Bambi* or somethin'," the man called after them.

"Shhh!" at least three dozen people said.

Outside on the sidewalk, Chelsey leaned against the building and laughed until tears rolled down her cheeks. Mitch rubbed his mangled arm and scowled, then a smile tugged at the corners of his mouth and slowly spread into a wide grin.

"You're so cuckoo," he said, chuckling, "You're going to get us thrown in jail someday."

"Did you see the teeth on that alligator? I bet he gobbled that guy up."

"Don't be silly, they don't eat heroes!"

"No?"

"No."

"Oh. Well, that's reassuring."

"I wonder if *Bambi* is showing anywhere in town," Mitch said.

"Now that is a scary movie." Chelsey shook her head. "There's this fire in the forest, you know, and Thumper and all those guys are—"

"What kind of nightmares will you have if I take you bowling?"

"I think that's safe enough," she said merrily.

"Forget it, I hate to bowl. I was just checking, that's all. Let's go have an ice-cream soda."

"I had this dream once about a giant straw and an ice-cream scoop that were chasing me and—"

Mitch's kiss silenced Chelsey's nonsense and muffled the bubble of laughter in her throat. Oh, my, she was happy. She'd never know how the movie ended and she didn't care. She was with Mitch, her hero, her Prince Charming, and she was safe and protected in his strong embrace. Even alligators knew enough not to hassle heroes!

At a café near the theater they ordered double chocolate sodas. While they were waiting someone called her name, and Chelsey looked up to see Tony Harrison and his flight attendant walking over to them. Introductions were made but Tony refused the invitation to sit down, saying they were headed for the late movie.

"Great," Chelsey said, "you can tell me how it ends."

"Why didn't you stay?" Tony asked.

"It was too scary for Mitch."

"Oh, man," Mitch said, rolling his eyes.

Tony laughed. "I sympathize, Brannon. I took her to a James Bond once and she nearly pulled my arm out of the socket."

"The circulation is just now coming back," Mitch said, peering at his muscular arm, which the flight attendant also seemed to find quite fascinating.

"Say, Chels, your work on the lumberyard project is great. You can have as much overtime as you want."

"She won't be doing that anymore, Harrison," Mitch said. "I'm surprised you agreed to it in the first place since you claim to be Chelsey's friend. Couldn't you see she was out on her feet?"

"Yeah, I knew that, but I figured she'd go be a waitress or something if I turned her down."

"Just remember," Mitch said, "she leaves at closing from now on."

"Sure." Tony nodded. "I understand, Brannon."

"Do you?" Mitch looked directly at Tony. "There's nothing else that needs discussing?"

"I'm reading you loud and clear," Tony said. "About everything."

"Good."

"Well, see ya," Tony said and hurried his date toward the door.

"Mitch, you were threatening Tony," Chelsey said. "You told him to stay away from me."

"I said you wouldn't be working overtime."

"You were delivering more of a message than that, Mitch Brannon."

"Me?" He smiled innocently.

"Tony turned white!"

"Maybe he isn't feeling well."

"Mitch!"

"Look," he said, reaching across the table and taking her hand, "it needed saying. Harrison now knows he's not taking you out anymore. You are *my* lady, Chelsey. I don't share. Hell, I should have decked him for letting you have that extra work. The guy is a jerk."

"Actually he's very nice, but I won't argue the point," Chelsey said. "His date was dippy though."

"She'd do in a pinch."

"She was practically drooling on your shirt front!" Chelsey said, waggling a finger at him. "I gave her four dirty looks and she completely ignored me."

"It's all in the way you communicate, my sweet. Harrison and I reached an instant understanding."

"You did your hitman routine. I won't tell Patsy, though."

"Chelsey," Mitch said softly, "you *are* mine. I hope you don't have a problem with that."

"No, Mitch," she said, smiling warmly, "no problem at all."

On the way home they debated loudly as to whether stars twinkle or wink. Mitch opened the back door at Chelsey's and stepped aside while Zork gave Myrtle her free ride inside.

"Everyone is present and accounted for," he said, back in the living room.

"May I offer you coffee, fruit, or—"

"You?" he said, pulling her into his arms. "I'd like a nice serving of a very lengthy good night kiss."

"Mitch, thank you so much for taking such good care of me when I was so tired. It's been a very long time since there was anyone to pamper me."

"All part of the service. As they say at the movies, 'Shhh.'"

He lowered his head and took possession of her mouth, kissing her hard and long as their tongues met in the ice-cream-flavored sweet regions of their mouths. His hands slid down over her buttocks, drawing her up against the rugged length of his body where his arousal became immediately evident. Chelsey trailed her fingertips over his muscular back, drinking in the feel of his strength, the raw power he was holding tightly in check.

Desire surged through her as Mitch's thumbs flickered across the tips of her breasts. Instantly they grew taut and throbbing and she remembered the ecstasy from the night by the pool when his mouth had sought and found the ivory mounds and filled her with a raging flame of passion. She wanted once again to sink her fingers into the tawny hair on his chest, feel the heat emanating from his bronzed skin.

"Chelsey," Mitch murmured as he placed nibbling kisses down her slender throat.

"Oh, Mitch."

"I'll . . . see you after lunch tomorrow," he said, his voice strained. "Sleep well, my lady." He kissed her gently on the forehead and slowly stepped away from her.

Voices seemed to scream through Chelsey's mind. She wanted Mitch, she did! She loved him and ached for the fulfillment his body would bring her. All she had to do was reach out her hand, lead him to the bedroom . . .

But she was frozen in place, unable to move, speak, or hardly breathe. She simply looked up at him. He smiled and fleetingly caressed her cheek, then turned and quietly left the house. The sound of the truck's engine snapped her out of her trancelike state, and she spun around in the direction of the noise.

Dear Lord, what was wrong with her? She had let Mitch disappear into the night, leaving her alone and awash with desire. Had he been angry because she hadn't taken him to her bed? No, his smile had been a loving, visual embrace, a gentle good night. What was he thinking? What was *she* thinking? Her mind and body seemed to be operating on two separate planes, each taking independent actions beyond her control.

Why? Why? Why hadn't she made love with Mitch Brannon? She had been so sure the mental turmoil was over, that she had found her inner peace and knew with no reservation what she wanted, what she would do. Then why hadn't she, for Pete's sake?

"Oh, Zork," she said, blinking back her tears of confusion, "what is the matter with me? I love Mitch so why don't I . . . you know? Oh, hell, I'm going to sleep."

Chelsey slept restlessly and awoke groggy and out of sorts. After a shower and a breakfast of coffee and fresh fruit she felt halfway human.

"Chelsey, are you in there?" a voice yelled.

"Hi, Polly," Chelsey said, opening the door.

"Is it safe?" Polly whispered. "I mean, Mitch's truck isn't here, so . . ."

"Come in, Polly."

"Are you sure?"

"Polly!"

"I'm in," Polly said, bouncing into the room and sinking onto the sofa. "So! How's life?"

"Fine."

"Fine? You've got a lover that looks like a centerfold and all you can say is, 'fine'? I swear, Chelsey, that Mitch is the most incredible man I have ever seen. I could have some very naughty thoughts about him, but I won't 'cause he's yours. Annie is so excited because Mitch spent the night with you."

"Well, he did but he didn't," Chelsey said miserably, sinking onto the rocker.

"What does that mean?"

"Polly, I—we didn't . . . you know."

"Why the hell not? Are you nuts? Are you saying he stayed here and nothing happened? Chelsey, this is Polly, your dear friend. You don't have to pretend for me. I mean, well, if I had a guy like that who wanted to—"

"We did not make love!"

"Does one of you have a problem I don't know about?"

"I'm not sure," Chelsey said. "The whole thing is up to me, you see, and I just fizzled out, stood there like a rock and said a fond farewell. Sick. Really sick."

"Mitch is letting you decide if you're going to . . . you know?"

"Yes."

"My goodness," Polly said, "I'm not sure I'd like that. I think it would be better to get all carried away in the throes of passion and then take equal responsibility afterward. That's a heavy number to take on alone."

"Tell me about it," Chelsey said, frowning.

"You know, Mitch isn't playing fair. Why doesn't he just seduce the hell out of you and get it over with?"

"Well, see, we had this long talk and he said I had control over my own body."

"Nice gesture, but it puts you in a very bad place. When I take that step I want someone to be mad at just in case I have an adverse reaction to what I did. Know what I mean? I'm not having some guy telling me it was all my fault. So what are you going to do?"

"I have no idea. I think I know and then it turns out I didn't know and—Polly, I'm in love with Mitch!"

"Oh, sweetie, you found your Prince Charming." Polly smiled happily. "That's so great. Does he love you?"

"No, he hasn't said so. He really cares for me though. He calls me his lady and made it very clear to Tony that Mr. Harrison is to stay out of the picture."

"How macho and classy. I bet Tony shook in his shoes."

"He was rather gray around the edges. Anyway, the point is, I know I'm in love with Mitch so why am I acting like such an idiot? He's everything I've been waiting for."

"Not quite," Polly said, shaking her head. "You and I are an endangered species, Chelsey. We want it all."

"Meaning?"

"The returned love of the man we finally give ourselves to, a lifetime commitment, station wagons, babies, and PTA meetings."

"In this day and age?"

"So we're in the wrong decade or century." Polly shrugged. "It's not our fault we're behind the liberated times."

"Well, I plan to catch up!" Chelsey said fiercely.

"Betcha you don't. You can't change who you are and what you believe in. Am I depressing you?"

"I may slit my throat."

"Gosh, I'm sorry. Let's cut your hair."

"What?"

"Whenever I get the gloom and dooms, I change my hairstyle. It works wonders for my morale."

"No, I don't think so."

"Oh, come on. I'll just trim it a bit. It's such a gorgeous color and has those natural waves. It'll be great, you'll see."

"I'm so desperate, I'll try anything." Chelsey sighed. "Why don't you operate on my brain while you're at it?"

"Would if I could, but I'm afraid you're stuck with Chelsey Star as she is."

"Blak!"

An hour later, Chelsey peered into the mirror and smiled. Polly had done a marvelous job. Chelsey's hair was feathered into soft curls around her face and layered in the back to fall to her shoulders in natural waves.

"Well?" Polly asked.

"I love it! Thank you. Do you think I look older, more worldly?"

"No."

"Damn. I do like it, though, and I'm definitely cheered up."

"Good. I've got to dash, kiddo. If you need to talk, remember I'm around. I hope you work this thing out with Mitch because that might mean you and I aren't so weird after all. Do you think we're the only two virgins over twenty-one in San Diego?"

"No, I think we claim that dubious honor for the entire state of California."

"Really? How awful! I'm going home to cut my hair. 'Bye."

Just as Polly left the house, the telephone rang and Chelsey said hello cheerfully.

"Hello," a male voice said, "this is Mike Brannon. May I speak to Zork, please?"

"Pardon me?"

"This is Michael Mitchell Brannon, and I really need to talk to Zork."

"Michael Mitchell, or Mitchell Michael?"

"Michael Mitchell, the older, more intelligent, better looking of the Brannon boys."

"Oh, *that* Michael Mitchell." Chelsey laughed. "Well, I'm sorry but Zork is watching a baseball game on television and refuses to come to the phone. May I take a message?"

"Yes, I wish to express my sincere apologies for doubting his existence."

"Oh?'

"I am now the recipient of twenty pictures of the Great Dane in question, complete with sunglasses securely in place. There's even a shot of him eating a cat."

"He's not eating her! He carries Myrtle around like that."

"So I've been told by the lunatic who is presently holding a gun to my head, threatening me with bodily harm if I don't make amends to Zork."

"Well, I'll relay your expression of remorse, Michael Mitchell, but I can't guarantee that Zork will forgive you. He's extremely sensitive."

"Beg and plead! I'm a married man with starving children and I'm too young to die. Please, Chelsey, my life is in your hands."

"I'll see what I can do," she said, laughing uncontrollably.

"Bless you, child. Oh, Mitchell Michael wants to talk to you. Make it quick though, because the guys in the white coats will be here any minute to cart him away."

"Got it."

"Chelsey?"

"Hi, Mitch. You've flipped your cork, huh?"

"I certainly did not!" he said indignantly. "Mike is just a sore loser."

"Are you actually holding a gun to his head?"

"It's a plastic squirt gun, but he's so dumb he can't tell the difference."

"Is Michael Mitchell really better looking than you?"

"Lord, no! He's ugly as sin. He's got these gross muscles all over the place, naturally curly hair, and was homecoming king in college. I don't know how his wife can stand him."

"As someone once said, it sounds like he'd do in a pinch."

Mitch sighed. "There's no accounting for taste. Well, see you in an hour, babe."

"Okay."

" 'Bye."

The Brannons were whacko and wonderful, Chelsey thought as she hung up the receiver. What a fun family. They carried on with their nonstop nonsense and yet it was apparent how much they all loved each other. And now she loved a Brannon too. What ecstasy it would be to stand by Mitch's side as his wife and be gathered into the fold of the Brannons. But for Chelsey to have that place, Mitch would have to love her, want to commit himself to her for the rest of his life, and he had given no hint of any such plans for their future.

Was that the root of her hesitancy to make love with Mitch? Was she really subconsciously blackmailing him into expressing undying love in exchange for her body? What a disgusting thought. She wasn't that sort of person. Was she? Or was it true and so deeply encased in her basic makeup she'd never be able to change?

Surely she could rise above her antiquated values and live for the moment, for what she could share with Mitch. For if she didn't, she had a chilling feeling in her heart that she would lose him. Mitch's patience and restraint must be running out. She was living on borrowed time in her rosy world with him.

"Now I'm depressed again," she said to a sleeping Zork. "I will not, however, cut off any more of my hair."

Mitch whistled low and long when he arrived and saw Chelsey's new coiffeur. He turned her slowly around, nodding in approval.

"Sharp. Really nice," he said.

"Polly did it, and I'm glad you approve, sir."

"I do indeed," he said, tangling his fingers in the auburn tresses.

"Don't mess it up! I'm supposed to be gorgeous."

"You"—he kissed her—"are"—he kissed her again—"beautiful." He added one more for good measure.

"That great, huh?" she said, patting her hair.

"I'd better shut up or you'll get as conceited as my brother."

She laughed. "You two are dangerous together. I mean, you are really, really strange."

"It runs in the family, remember? I knew I'd hitched up with a weird outfit when I found out what they had named us. Oh, by the way, my mother isn't mad at me anymore. She's pleased I found you again. That lady has a wild temper when she gets going, but I'm back in her good graces. She still wants us to come over for dinner soon and I said I'd ask you."

"That sounds very nice."

"She makes terrific potatoes. Ready to go shopping?"

"I don't know, Mitch. I'm not sure I should spend money on furniture."

"Doesn't cost anything to browse. Come on."

The store he had selected, Mitch said, was neither too expensive nor too junky. It was right in the middle and had a wide variety to choose from. Chelsey's eyes were sparkling with excitement as they wandered through the attractive groupings. She had never in her life owned anything as lovely as what was on display. Her parents had never been able to afford anything but secondhand furnishings for their home, and Chelsey's house was also made up of items purchased at thrift shops.

"Oh, Mitch," she said, "it's all so—so new."

He chuckled softly and kissed her on the forehead.

"Try this one," he said, leading her to a tweed chair with a matching sofa.

Chelsey sat on the plush cushion and ran her hand over the fabric, which was a combination of orange, brown, and green in perfectly matched tones. She leaned back and closed her eyes, relishing the feel of the chair as it seemed to wrap itself around her.

"Heavenly," she said. "Don't tell me how much it costs."

"Well—um—these tickets are wrong because they're having a sale."

"How do you know that?" she asked, squinting up at him.

"It was in the paper. I'll go ask the clerk what the price is now." He strode away.

"Too much, that's what," Chelsey said, cringing as she looked at the tag.

When Mitch returned he was grinning. "Half price," he said.

"You're kidding. Why?"

"They need the room for an incoming shipment or something. Do you want it?"

"Oh, yes! I can't believe they're reducing it that much. It's fantastic."

"Look, Chelsey, I'll put this on my credit card and you can write me a check when we get back to the house."

"Why?"

"Because you haven't put the loan money in your account yet and it might not clear in time to cover it."

"I never thought of that."

"You sit there and enjoy, and I'll go do the paperwork."

"Okay."

Chelsey snuggled further into the chair as Mitch headed for the front desk.

"May I help you?" a woman asked.

"Oh, no, thank you," Chelsey said. "We've decided on this set. You people certainly have super sales."

"That advertised special ended yesterday, dear. Everything is back to the prices on the tags."

"What?" Chelsey said, jumping to her feet.

"I'm sorry, dear, but—"

"Mitch Brannon," Chelsey yelled, stomping over to the counter where he was standing, "you just hold it."

"Just a sec, babe. I have to sign this thing and—"

"I want to talk to you!"

"Yeah, okay, in a minute."

"Now!"

"Pregnant women are very emotional," Mitch said to the nervous clerk before hauling Chelsey several feet away. "What is your problem?" he asked, scowling.

"That furniture is not on sale."

"You don't say," he said, eyebrows raised in innocence.

"You lied!"

"No, I stretched the truth and made the sale last an extra day."

"Why?"

"Because we're compromising again but I forgot to tell you. Well, now you know, so everything's fine."

"It certainly is not!"

"Chelsey, you can't expect to have your own way all the time. It's simply not fair."

"Huh?"

"See, I want to buy this stuff for you up front, from me

to you. Since you probably won't go for that we'll strike a middle ground and each pay half. It's a brilliant plan and acceptable to both parties involved. In the excitement of the moment I just forgot to mention how this was being done. Get it?"

"I—"

"Good."

"No, Mitch. I am footing the whole bill or—"

"Hush, dear," he said, kissing her quickly. "Don't upset yourself. You must remember your condition."

"My what?"

He grinned. "You're pregnant, if you recall."

"Oh, for heaven's sake." She marched away and flopped back down in her chair. She couldn't let Mitch pay for half the furniture, she thought. Talk about always getting your own way. He was spoiled rotten. Well, she'd tackle this again when they got back to the house.

Chelsey could hardly contain her exuberance as the sofa and chair were loaded onto the back of Mitch's truck. At her house, Mitch rounded up a couple of teenage boys he had met while riding the bike, and between them they carried the furniture inside. The boys stated that Chelsey's old sofa was in better shape than the one they had and toted it off down the block.

"Now!" Chelsey said, turning on Mitch. "About the money. I know what this cost and—"

"Please, babe," he said, "fifty-fifty, okay?"

"Mitch, I . . ."

"Please?"

"Okay." She sighed. "You win, but then you always do."

"Don't be silly. We have a very equal relationship."

"Oh, ha!"

Chelsey carefully made out a check payable to Mitch for the amount he quoted, then she stretched out on the new sofa, grinning broadly.

"Oh, my," she said, "it's so—so . . . I'm acting silly."

"No," he said quietly, sitting down next to her, "you're not. You're overdue to have nice things. You've waited a long time and worked very hard. It's your turn, Chelsey. Your responsibility for Richard is taken care of and you're going to concentrate on you. You owe it to yourself."

"It was your money, Mitch."

"A loan, and that has nothing to do with it. What's important is that you enjoy it, live a little. Promise me you'll do that."

She frowned. "Why are you being so serious?"

"Promise?"

"Yes, all right. I'll—um—I'll buy a new dress."

"Perfect. That's the kind of thing I'm talking about. This room really looks nice. We, my lady, have excellent taste."

"In furniture?"

"Among other things," he said, and leaned over and kissed her deeply.

Chelsey circled his neck with her arms to draw him closer and the kiss intensified. Mitch lifted his head for a moment and stretched out next to her, wrapping his arm around her waist and molding her to the contours of his body.

Their rapacious mouths met again and their breathing became labored as heartbeats quickened. Again Chelsey could feel Mitch holding himself in tight control, his muscles trembling under the onslaught of his rising passion. She couldn't continue to do this to him! It wasn't fair to him to offer just a portion of herself. She had to meet his needs or lose him altogether.

"Oh, babe," Mitch said, his hand roaming over her back.

"Chelsey! Mitch!" Polly's voice screamed from the box on the wall. "It's Annie! She's fallen and—oh, God!"

Mitch was on his feet and barreling out the front door so quickly that Chelsey was still struggling to sit up. She ran after him and they entered Annie's living room together.

"Oh, Lord," Polly said, "she's unconscious. I came over to bring her some cupcakes, and—and—"

Mitch dropped to his knees beside the tiny, frail woman who lay unmoving on the floor. He checked her pulse and gently moved his hands over her arms and legs.

"Mitch?" Chelsey whispered.

"Call an ambulance," he said. "I think she's broken her hip."

"I'll do it," Polly said. "Oh, our poor Annie."

"Annie?" Mitch said. "Come on, gorgeous, wake up."

"That you, Golden Boy?" Annie said, her voice weak.

"You bet. We're taking you to the hospital and everything is going to be fine."

"Chelsey? Polly?" Annie whispered.

"They're right here too. We all are, Annie."

"Then I'm happy," she said. "Over and out."

It was late that night before Chelsey, Polly, and Mitch climbed out of the truck in Chelsey's driveway.

"Thank you, Mitch," Polly said, hugging him tightly. "You were wonderful. I was a basket case. Good night, both of you."

" 'Night," Chelsey and Mitch said.

In her house Chelsey collapsed wearily onto the sofa and rested her head on the top.

"Annie looked so tiny in that bed, Mitch," she said.

"She's going to be fine. Her hip will just take awhile longer to mend because of her arthritis."

"Polly was right. You were wonderful. It meant so much to Annie to have you there."

"She's a nifty old gal. Now, you are going to bed. We just got you all rested up and you're not undoing our good work."

"Maybe I'll sleep on my new sofa."

"Whatever, as long as you do it pronto. I'll call you tomorrow night." He kissed her quickly.

"Don't you ever run out of . . . uh, niceness?"

"I think you made that word up. Now sexiness I can understand. Good night, babe."

" 'Night, Mitch."

Chelsey did indeed spend the night on her beautiful new sofa which confused Myrtle terribly. The cat kept wandering back and forth and finally slept right in the middle of the double bed. In the morning, Chelsey called the hospital and was told that Annie had had a peaceful night's rest and was presently eating her breakfast.

"We all love her," the nurse said. "Don't worry about a thing. Oh, over and out."

Chelsey laughed. "Over and out."

She walked to the bank and deposited Mitch's check in the automatic teller machine, then caught the bus for work.

"Hi, Tony," she said as she passed him in the corridor.

"I've never seen you before in my life," he said.

"What's *your* problem?"

"Hey, Mitch Brannon has muscles on his muscles and apparently has no aversion to using them. He'd make mincemeat out of me. I love ya, darlin', but not enough to get myself killed."

"He wouldn't hit you! Well, maybe he would. I don't know."

"It's serious between you two, huh, Chels?"

"I—I love him, Tony, but I'm not entirely sure how he feels about me."

"I was there! He's ready to do battle for you. I guess I was wrong about him. He definitely is a one-woman man."

"But for how long?" she said softly.

"That's the biggy, Chels, and only time will tell. I just hope you don't get hurt. Do me a favor. If he asks, I absolutely did not speak to you."

She laughed. "Are you not brave?"

"What I are, is smart!"

"Oh, Tony, Annie broke her hip. She's in Mercy Hospital."

"Dammit, no kidding? Is she going to be all right?"

"Yes, but it sure was scary. Mitch just took charge and got her the help she needed."

"I'm going to end up liking him and I really don't want to. I'll send Annie some flowers today."

"She'll love that. See you later."

"Only in the shadows. Never in public. I want to live to be an old, sexually active man. Chels?"

"Yes?"

"Do you think maybe this guy is your Prince Charming?"

"Oh, Tony, I hope so."

"Me too, sweetheart. I like seeing you happy. By the way, your hair looks great."

"I adore you, Tony."

"Would you be quiet? Brannon's rich enough to afford undercover agents. Cripes!" He stalked away as Chelsey laughed and headed for her cubicle.

"Undercover agents?" a voice yelled. "What happened to the bagels?"

Chelsey received so many compliments on her new hairstyle during the day that she was feeling borderline beautiful by the time she arrived home. She fed Zork and Myrtle, called the hospital to check on Annie, and changed into shorts and a lightweight summer sweater. The telephone rang as she was heading for the kitchen and she retraced her steps to answer it cheerfully.

"Hi, babe."

"Hello, Mitchell Michael."

"Before I forget, we sent Annie some flowers."

"Oh, Mitch, how thoughtful. I was going to take her some when I could get over to the hospital, but this is even better."

"I signed the card 'Chelsey and Golden Boy' because I wasn't sure she'd know who Mitch was."

"Excellent thinking."

"Chelsey, I have good news and bad news."

"Uh-oh."

"Good news is that Saturday night I am taking you wining, dining, and dancing, which will call for that new dress you intend to buy."

"Marvelous. And the bad bulletin?"

"I'll be out of town until then."

"Oh, no! Where are you going?"

"Mike and I have to go up to San Francisco to check out some land. It'll take several days since we have to investigate the zoning restrictions, water access, all that junk. You know that nasty man who was with my mother at the restaurant?"

"That was your father!"

"Yeah, him. This is all his fault. I told him I would never speak to him again, but he said that was the best headline he'd had in a month, so that didn't get me anywhere at all."

"Are you pouting?"

"Damn right I am. I'm going to miss you, Chelsey Star. I'm going to miss you a helluva lot!"

"And I will certainly miss you. Can you come over tonight?"

"No, we're driving up in an hour because we have a meeting scheduled first thing in the morning. Can you believe this? I'm being sabotaged by my own father! I'm plotting my revenge, though."

"Oh, dear."

"He hates broccoli. I mean, Frank Brannon can't be in the same room with the stuff. So next year on my birthday . . ."

"You'll order a dinner made up totally of broccoli." Chelsey laughed. "You're a rotten kid, Brannon."

"He's got it coming. Dammit, I better go get packed. Chelsey, please take good care of yourself while I'm away. Lord, I am hating this! I'll call you tomorrow night."

"All right, Mitch. I'll be looking forward to Saturday night very, very much. Drive carefully."

" 'Bye, babe. Chelsey?"

"Yes?"

"I—good-bye."

"Good night, Mitch."

Chelsey hung up the receiver and was frowning as she walked slowly into the kitchen. Darn that Frank Brannon. The man did have a business to run, but still . . . Mitch was so uptight, it was almost funny. Broccoli for his birthday dinner! He'd probably do it too! When he had said he would miss her there had been a near franticness in his voice, a sound of frustration. His feelings for her were growing, she knew they were! How much control did a man like Mitch have over his emotions? Was he capable of continually stopping short of falling in love and bailing out quickly? Had he become adept at sidestepping a commitment and disappearing when danger signals appeared?

"What does Mitch want from life, Zork?" Chelsey asked the dog, who wagged his tail vigorously. "That, my friend, is the unanswered question of the year."

When Chelsey opened her eyes the next morning, she instantly missed Mitch. That was silly, she thought as she ate breakfast. She didn't see him first thing in the morning anyway, but she knew he was in San Francisco and not just across town and that seemed to make a depressing difference.

An unexpected knock at the front door produced a smiling man in jeans, work shirt, and a hard hat.

"Chelsey Star?" he said.

"Yes."

"Mitch Brannon, my boss, asked me to bring his truck by for you to use while he's out of town. He said you're to drive it to work and something about visiting Annie Oakley. I sure hope you know what that means."

"Yes, I do, but I can't drive a truck!"

"He mentioned you might say that, ma'am." The man chuckled. "Mitch said to tell you that anyone who can impersonate Reggie Jackson like you do, can surely handle a pickup. Here's the keys. My buddy is out at the curb to pick me up. Nice meeting you, ma'am."

"Thank you very much. I appreciate your coming all the way over here."

"Like I said, Mitch is the boss. But I don't mind telling you I've been mighty interested in seeing the Chelsey Star we've all been hearing so much about. Now I know why Mitch has his head in the clouds. You're a pretty, pretty little thing."

"Well, I . . . well, thank you."

"Have a nice day, ma'am. Say, do you really have a Great Dane named Zork that wears sunglasses?"

"Yes." Chelsey laughed. "I do."

"Damn, I bet the other way. Lost ten bucks on that

one. Mike Brannon was so sure that Mitch had a screw loose. Oh, well. See ya."

Mitch had been telling his men about her? Chelsey thought wildly as she closed the door and stared at the keys in her hand. He had his head in the clouds? *In the clouds?* Mitch Brannon? And what a dear, sweet thing to do, having his truck delivered to her. How could Mitch say and do all the wonderful things he did and not be in love with her? It all added up to love. It did! But, dammit, why didn't he tell her? Unless he wasn't in love with her and always went all-out in a relationship while it lasted. Talk about a depressing thought! She'd better stop thinking about it or she'd end up cutting her hair again. At the rate she was going, she'd be bald and would have to wear her baseball cap forever.

"Like Reggie Jackson," she said suddenly. "The Ferrari! The windshield! When is Mitch going to get that thing fixed?"

Seven

Driving a truck was a snap, Chelsey decided. Well, once you got the hang of it. Oh, what luxury to whiz right out of your own driveway and not have to hike to the bus stop. As for the speeding ticket she had gotten, she'd simply explain to Mitch that the gas pedal had been a bit tricky at first but she had figured it out . . . eventually.

"Chels, please," Tony had begged, "let me get all the way out of the parking lot tonight before you even put the key in the ignition. I saw you barrel in and I aged before my very eyes."

"Oh, pooh!" Chelsey said, sticking her nose in the air and flouncing away.

When she screeched into the driveway that evening, Polly was waiting for her.

"Hi, Polly," she said, sliding out of the cab of the truck. "Like my mean machine?"

"I thought I saw you doing wheelies this morning and wanted to check. Where's marvelous Mitch?"

"He had to go to San Francisco and left the truck for

me to use. Fun, huh? Hey, come in and have dinner and then we'll go visit Annie."

"Great. I'll drive us in my car."

"No! We'll go in the truck."

"Chelsey, I terrify easily!"

"Don't be silly. I'm getting very good at zooming around in this thing. You'll be fine."

"Yeah, right," Polly said with a frown as she followed Chelsey into the house. "Wow! Look at this! My gosh, your furniture is beautiful. But how . . . Chelsey, did Mitch buy this for you?"

"No, not exactly. He was very upset because I was working overtime and having to worry about Richard. Anyway, he loaned me some money and I signed a note. It's all strictly business. He cheated a little on the furniture, though. Sit down and try it out while I feed Zork and Myrtle."

Polly was still frowning when Chelsey came back into the living room.

"Don't you think it's comfortable?" Chelsey asked.

"What? Oh, it's super. It's just that—oh, forget it. I'm probably just reading this wrong."

"What do you mean?"

"Did Mitch suggest you use some of the money to buy this stuff?"

"Well, yes. He even took me shopping."

"That bum! You didn't . . . you know, yet, did you?"

"No. What is wrong with you, Polly?"

"Chelsey, if a man is planning to carry you off to his cave for the rest of your lives, why would he urge you to fix up your own place? I'm sure Mitch doesn't need an extra sofa and chair at his house."

"No, he doesn't," Chelsey said, sinking onto the rocker. "He said it was my turn to have nice things."

"Yeah, yours not his. Prince Charming just turned back into a frog, Chelsey. The writing is on the wall. Oh, he cares for you, that much is evident, but he obviously has no program to take you away from all this. He's pushing you to make it better so he won't have a guilty conscience when he—"

"Leaves me?" Chelsey said, jumping to her feet. "Is that what you think this is all about? He fixes my roof, brings in enough food for a battalion, even artichoke hearts, decks out my living room like *House Beautiful* and takes a hike?"

"The signs are all there," Polly said sadly.

"No, Polly, you're wrong! Aren't you? Of course you are. Aren't you? Mitch even told his workmen about me."

"But why the big number to spruce up your humble abode?"

"I don't know. Why do you have to think so much?"

"Someone around here has to keep a clear head. You're in love, so can't be expected to do that. Love turns brains into oatmeal. Hey, it would be wonderful if I'm wrong, but . . ."

"But it doesn't look too good," Chelsey said miserably.

"Nope."

"Oh, damn. Let's eat. I can't handle this."

"If you're depressed we can always—"

"You are not cutting my hair!"

"Whatever." Polly shrugged. "I'm sorry if I upset you, but I had to tell it as I see it."

"You sound like a newscaster."

"Well, you are my best friend, Chelsey, and you're so dewy-eyed over Mitch you aren't facing facts. I'm trying to make sure you stay . . . alert to these little subtle hints he's tossing out. In my opinion, though, this one is more like a neon sign with a flashing message."

"I'm going to cry."

"Later, okay? We have to visit Annie."

"And buy me a new dress."

"What for?"

"Mitch is taking me to a special place Saturday night when he gets back and said I should get a fancy outfit. What does that mean?"

"Nothing," Polly said, smiling. "He simply wants to show you off. I'm not saying he's totally rotten. He was wonderful when Annie got hurt. He's a nice, nice man, Chelsey, he really is. I just don't think he's the marrying kind, doesn't want a long-term commitment. He's making certain that your life is in order before he disappears into the sunset. Actually that's extremely decent of him."

"Ugh."

"It is! Not many guys would bother. What you have to decide is whether or not you want to sleep with him before it's over. I don't think you'll be able to do it, but it's up to you."

"I don't want it to be over!" Chelsey wailed. "I love him."

"I know, dear friend. How are you at living off of fond memories?"

"Oh, hell!"

"Thought so. What's to eat around here?"

Chelsey refused to discuss any further Mitch's ulterior motives for insisting that she glamorize her house, and even managed to push the whole thing to the back of her mind for the time being. After dinner, she and Polly headed for the hospital, Polly hanging onto the seat for dear life as Chelsey whipped the truck through the traffic.

Annie was delighted to see them, proudly showed off her pretty flowers, and had them sign her cast with a blue crayon. They hugged her good-bye, laughed when Annie waved and said, "Over and out," and headed for a shopping mall.

"Sexy, frilly, frumpy, what?" Polly asked, looking at the selection of dresses.

"Medium sexy," Chelsey said. "Halfway between the high school prom and obscene."

"Got it. Oh, Chelsey, here it is! Oh! It's perfect. Try it on."

The creation was a kelly green satin gown that accentuated Chelsey's auburn hair and glowing tan. It was cut low over her breasts, hugged her waist and slender hips.

"Oh, Chelsey," Polly whispered, "you're . . . beautiful."

"Really? It's a bit . . . daring," Chelsey said, trying to

tug the material up more over her breasts. "I'm falling out of the top."

"I should have such problems. It's perfect. I hope it comes with a big stick."

"A what?"

"To beat off Muscles Mitch. He's going to die on the spot or turn into an octopus."

"Interesting thought."

"You talk brave, but what happens when he pounces on your bones when he sees you in this?"

"I'll worry about that later."

"The ostrich and the octopus." Polly laughed. "Sounds like the title of a book."

"Don't mention books. Reminds me of Cinderella."

"And Prince Charming?"

"Yeah, him." Chelsey frowned. "I think Cinderella got the last one they made."

"We'll have him cloned."

The elegant gown was purchased and placed in layers of tissue in a gold box and the pair returned to Chelsey's.

" 'Bye," Polly said in the driveway.

"Aren't you coming in?"

"I have to go home and calm my jangled nerves. You drive like a lunatic!"

"Thanks a bunch!"

"Chelsey, I'm really sorry if I upset you by what I said about Mitch."

"I know, it was for my own good. I appreciate your concern, Polly. See you tomorrow."

" 'Bye."

Chelsey carefully hung the green dress in the closet, then carried a huge bunch of grapes to the sofa. Her mouth was full when the telephone rang and she mumbled her hello.

"Chelsey? Is that you?"

"I'm wheating!"

"What?"

Chelsey chomped on the grapes and swallowed them nearly whole.

"I'm eating." She laughed. "Hi, Mitch."

"Hi, babe. I called earlier but I guess you were visiting Annie."

"Yep. Polly went with me. Oh, thank you for the use of the truck. I'm having a grand time with it."

"Did you dent a fender yet?"

"Of course not! You know, the police in this town are really nice."

"The what?"

"The one that gave me the ticket was a—"

"Ticket?"

"For speeding. It wasn't my fault, though, because the gas pedal is weird and—"

"Oh, man," Mitch said, whooping with laughter. "I'm hooked up with a felon."

"I am not! Change the subject. How are you?"

"Lonely," he said softly. "Missing you, Chelsey Star."

Polly was wrong, Chelsey thought frantically. If Mitch missed her, why would he leave her!

"Chelsey?"

"Yes, I'm here, and I wish you were."

"Are you sitting on your pretty new sofa?"

"Yes." Why did he have to mention the furniture! "How's San Francisco?"

"It's raining. I've been drenched to the skin all day, tromping around on soggy land. This trip is the pits. Tell me to come home."

"Come home."

"I'm on my way."

"Really?"

"No, dammit all, I'm stuck for the duration in the company of my obnoxious brother."

"Tsk, tsk, Mitchell Michael. I'm sure Michael Mitchell is very charming."

"Ha! I have to sleep in the same hotel room with him and he snores louder than Zork!"

"Goodness, that bad? Zork can rattle the windows."

"Don't you feel sorry for me, Chelsey?"

"Of course I do. I'll soothe your furrowed brow when you get back."

"That doesn't sound like much of an offer."

"No? Well, I'll give it some more thought."

"Are you eating good? Resting? Locking the doors
and—"

"Oh, good grief, yes!"

"Okay. I'd better go, Chelsey. I have to study a boring
tax report tonight. Do you suppose my father always
wanted a daughter and that's why he's treating me so
lousy?"

"Good night, silly man."

" 'Bye, pretty lady. I'll call you tomorrow. Stay out of
jail."

"I'll do my best."

"Sleep well, Chelsey mine. I—good night."

Chelsey slowly replaced the receiver and pressed her
fingertips to her temples. "Oh, Mitch," she whispered, "I
love you so much." If only, only she knew Mitch's true
feelings for her, the depth of his caring. She'd like to call
up his mother and ask Mrs. Brannon if her second-born
son always went into things at full tilt and then moved
on to the next project when his enthusiasm faded. She
had no way of knowing if this was Mitch's usual mode of
conduct when he was involved in a relationship. If it
was, there were a lot of broken hearts in San Diego,
California! For how could a woman not fall in love with
Mitch when he made her feel like the most important
person within his world?

But how long would she hold that place, command his
attention and care? Was Polly right? Was Mitch already
edging his way toward an exit, stage left? Did the loan,
the furniture, the mountain of groceries have the
unspoken message Polly had interpreted?

"How should I know?" Chelsey said angrily, getting to
her feet. "I'm only the woman who's in love with him!"

Late that night Chelsey wrote a letter to Richard,
explaining that she had decided to get a loan after all
and that he was not to worry about a thing. She
enclosed a check to cover his entire expenses for the
school year and stated very firmly that he was not to find
another job after his ankle had healed.

She made no reference to Mitch. As close as she and

Richard were she simply was not ready to share the existence of Mitch with her brother. Richard knew she was waiting for her Prince Charming and Polly kept insisting that Mitch was going to change into the frog! No, she'd inform Richard about Mitch later. If there was anything to tell.

When Mitch telephoned the next night he sneezed four times in rapid succession after saying hello.

"Mitch, are you messing around with someone's cat?" Chelsey asked.

"No, I caught a crummy cold. I'm dying, Chelsey. Come kiss me farewell."

"You really sound awful," she said, concerned.

"Yeah, I'm a wreck. The only good that has come of it is that Mike got his own room because he's afraid of my germs and I don't have to listen to him snore."

"See? Every cloud has a—"

"No, it doesn't."

"Goodness, you're crabby."

"Sorry, babe. How's Annie?"

"Everyone at the hospital adores her. Polly and I whizzed over in the truck and saw her after dinner."

"Whizzed? How much is that ticket going to cost you?"

"Cute. Mitch, I don't suppose you put the Ferrari in the shop so it could be fixed while you're away?"

"I didn't have time."

"Couldn't your father do it for you?"

"He doesn't have time either. How's Zork and Myrtle?"

They chatted for several more minutes, during which Mitch told her six times how much he missed her. His voice was low and husky, partially from the effects of his cold, and a delicious shiver of desire swept through Chelsey as his words caressed her like a velvet glove.

"Whew!" she said when she finally hung up. "Potent stuff!"

On Saturday morning, Chelsey cleaned her little house from front door to back, glancing often at her watch. Mitch had not been exactly sure what time he would return to San Diego, but had said their fancy date was definitely on. When he had called each night, his cold had been no better but he declared that nothing would keep them from their reunion celebration. When the telephone rang at six o'clock, Chelsey snatched it up.

"Hello."

"Chel"—Mitch sneezed—"sey?"

"Oh, Mitch, you really are ill. Are you home?"

"Yes, and I'll pick you up in an hour."

"Maybe you should stay in and take care of—"

"Seven o'clock," he growled.

"Yes, all right. Take an aspirin or something. Oh, Mitch, I'm so glad you're back."

"Me too, babe."

Chelsey nearly tripped over Zork as she ran into the bedroom, tugging her clothes loose as she went. She showered, shampooed, and blow-dried her hair, then took out the luscious green dress. A tingle of excitement swept through her as the creation floated into place over her slender figure.

It was beautiful! *She* was beautiful. The world was beautiful. And her Mitchell Michael Brannon would be arriving at any minute to sweep her into his strong arms. Beautiful!

"Mitch," Chelsey whispered as a knock sounded at the door, and she rushed to answer it.

As Mitch stepped into the room, Chelsey felt as if she couldn't breathe. They simply stood there, neither moving, as their eyes met and held in a warm, tender gaze. There were no such things as time, space, and reality. There was only the moment and it seemed to stretch into infinity.

"Oh, Chelsey," Mitch said finally, moving to her and cupping her face in his large hands. "I . . . I did miss you so much."

"Mitch, I—"

"Wait," he said, pulling a small bag out of the pocket of his perfectly cut black suit coat.

"What's this?" she said, accepting the offering.

"A bottle of Vitamin C tablets. I have to kiss you,

Chelsey. And I'm going to give you this cold for sure, so I want you to take these."

"Oh, Mitch." She laughed and tossed the package onto the sofa, then circled his neck with her arms. "I . . . adore you."

"That dress is sensational. You look fantastic and—oh, hell," he said, and kissed her fiercely.

Mitch was home, Chelsey thought dreamily as she returned the kiss with total abandonment. Oh, yes, her Mitch was home!

"Oh, Chelsey," he said, gathering her close to his chest. "You feel so good and I bet you smell good but my nose isn't working. Mike says if I mention your name again he's going to murder me because you were all I could talk about in San Francisco. I even missed Zork and Myrtle because they belong to you!"

"It seemed as though you were gone for weeks," Chelsey said.

"I know. We'd better go or we'll be late for our reservation. Man, that dress! Maybe you should wear a coat."

"It's hot outside!"

"Yeah, well, the first guy who takes a free eyeful is going to get a broken jaw!"

"My goodness."

"I mean it!"

"Would you rather I wore another dress?"

"No, this one's really something, but the something is mine! Zork, haul Myrtle out of here. My lady and I are doing the town tonight!"

Mitch had, to Chelsey's amazement, arrived in a taxi so he could drive his truck home later. It wasn't quite the vehicle he would have chosen for their gala evening, he said, but it would have to do. Chelsey offered to drive since she was such an expert, but Mitch declared that he'd prefer to live at least until his next birthday so he could execute his broccoli revenge upon his father.

The restaurant on Harbor Drive was one of San Diego's finest, and Chelsey's eyes widened at the splendor of the glittering chandeliers and velvet-cushioned chairs. They were seated at a cozy table that had a candle in the center. Chelsey gazed at Mitch's tanned, rugged face, his blond hair that changed colors in the flickering glow, and her heart nearly burst with love. Now she was complete, whole again. Now she could smile and laugh, for she was with Mitch.

He ordered an expensive champagne and toasted Chelsey with the bubbling liquid. They chose their meal from large flocked menus and Chelsey prided herself on the fact that she didn't gasp aloud when she saw the prices.

"Are you buying the property in San Francisco?" she asked pleasantly.

"We made an offer and should know in a few days. Please, no more talk of that particular city. It nearly killed me."

"You only have a cold."

"I was referring to missing you, Chelsey. You know, I think we should put Zork in guard dog school so you'll have some protection. We'll get him some of those mirrored sunglasses so he'll look cool and mean."

"No."

"Well, the least he could do is not smile all the time. I'll teach him how to scowl, okay? He'll appear more ominous."

She laughed. "Okay."

The food arrived and was delicious, but Chelsey frowned when she saw that Mitch hardly touched what was on his plate.

"Aren't you hungry?" she asked.

"I can't taste anything because of this cold," he said. "It's all the same flavor—nothing. Chelsey, remember when you told me you might change jobs when Richard graduated?"

"Yes."

"Well, his future is all set now and I wondered if you'd given that any more thought."

"Switching careers? No, not really."

"Don't you think you should?"

"Why?"

"Because you're not entirely happy where you are, and

it's time to be considering what you want to do with your life."

"Perhaps you have a point," she said, taking a deep breath. Dear God, Polly was right! Now Mitch even wanted to know that she was squared away in that area before—before he left her? No! Oh, Lord, no!

"Do you have any idea what direction you'd like to go?" Mitch asked.

Straight to his house as his wife, she thought wildly, and the mother of his babies! "It's—um—not that simple, Mitch."

"But you will think about it?"

"Yes."

"Good. Don't forget, it's your turn now. Your turn, Chelsey."

"To go to the ladies room," she said, forcing a smile. "I'll be right back, Mitch."

In the prettily furnished area, Chelsey sank onto a velvet-cushioned chair and pressed her hands to her cheeks. Why? she thought. Why was Mitch doing this? He was acting like a dying man who was getting his life in order before he disappeared from the face of the earth. Polly would consider Mitch's latest concern regarding Chelsey's future career plans another glaring warning of his pending exodus from her existence. Was Polly really so all-wise and knowing, or could she be wrong?

But how was Chelsey to know? The evidence was pointing more and more toward the conclusions Polly had drawn. Mitch seemed determined to cover every aspect of Chelsey's world, make sure it was secure, to her liking. Was he really preparing to leave her? But he had been so glad to see her after his trip, had held her in his arms as though he'd never again let her go. He had been frustrated and angry over their forced separation, almost desperate in his need to return to her side.

What was she going to do? Chelsey wondered. She couldn't waltz up to Mitch and casually ask him what in the heck his performance meant. She'd have to wait. Wait and see what the days ahead brought. In the meantime, Mitch was there and she loved him. For now, it would just have to do.

"Hello," she said, smiling when she rejoined Mitch at the table.

He scowled. "Don't do that again."

"Say hello?"

"No, don't walk across the room. Every bozo in the place was looking you over."

"Do not attack unless they touch."

"Ha! Would you like to go into the other room and dance?"

"Are you sure you feel well enough?"

"I dance with my feet, not my head."

"You should have a cold all the time, Mitch. Your voice is really sexy."

"No kidding?" He grinned. "Is it getting to you?"

"Oh, my, yes. I'm literally swooning."

Mitch chuckled and led Chelsey to a small ballroom. They found a table, ordered drinks, then moved onto the dance floor. Mitch caught Chelsey around the waist and pulled her against him, and she molded into the contours of his hard body with a contented sigh. Oh, he felt good, smelled so masculine, and she was nearly floating in ecstasy. He danced with practiced ease and grace, and Chesley was sure they were the most striking couple on the floor. She had seen the admiring glances Mitch had received from the women they passed and had felt a smug possessiveness. Mitch Brannon was hers! But for how long? No, she wouldn't spoil this blissful moment with gloomy thoughts.

He cradled her hand in his and brought it to his chest where she could feel the steady beating of his heart. He was so tall and strong and she was safely held in his protective embrace. His muscular thighs pressed against her and desire began to swirl through Chelsey. Her breasts grew taut as they brushed against his solid chest. He tipped his head to rest his lips lightly on her forehead and she closed her eyes, amazed at the powerful pleasure such a delicate gesture could bring.

Then Mitch sneezed. Not once, but six times, and the couples near them looked around in surprise.

"Heavens," Chelsey said, placing her hand on his cheek. "Mitch, you're burning up with fever."

He smiled. "That's what you do to me, hot stuff."

"We're going home."

"No way. I've been looking forward to this all week."

"Now!" she said, wiggling out of his arms and marching from the floor.

"Chelsey, for Pete's sake!" he yelled. "Oh, excuse me," he said to an enormous burly man who glared at him. "Chelsey," Mitch said when he caught up with her, "I don't want to leave yet."

"Mitch, when I was exhausted you issued orders like a drill sergeant. Now *you* are sick and I'm in charge. Haul it out of here, bub."

"Lord." He rolled his eyes to the heavens.

"Move!"

"Have you been taking lessons from my mother?"

"Go!"

Mitch muttered a few invectives that caused Chelsey's eyes to widen, but she stood firm in her resolve and minutes later they were in the truck and headed for her house. She would have preferred to chauffeur Mitch home, but after seeing his stormy expression decided not to press the issue.

"Now!" she said when they were in her living room. "Take off your jacket and tie."

"Anything else?" he said cockily.

"Your shoes!"

"Yes, ma'am."

"I'm going to fix you some hot lemonade."

"Gross. That sounds really gross."

"Tough. Sit down," she said, heading for the kitchen. She let Zork and Myrtle in from the yard, then set about her task.

When she returned to the living room with the steaming lemonade, her emotions were assaulted by a mixture of love, desire, and sympathy. Mitch had leaned his head back on the top of the sofa and closed his eyes.

A lock of his thick blond hair had tumbled over onto his forehead and his cheeks were flushed. He had pulled his white shirt loose from his pants and unbuttoned it, and she could see a fine film of perspiration glistening on his broad chest.

"Mitch, drink this," she said gently, sitting down next to him.

"I should take my germs home," he said, accepting the mug. "I'm sorry about this, Chelsey."

"As they say at the movies, 'Shhh.' "

"Hot lemonade, huh?" he said, peering into the cup.

"Bottoms up."

"Whose bottom?" He winked a soupy eye at her.

"I, sir, am the doctor in charge here. Now do as you're told."

"It's hot!"

"It's supposed to be! Lord, you're a big baby. I'll get you a pillow from the bed."

"Don't I get to go in there? I'm a sick man, Chelsey."

"Well, yes, I suppose so. Drink your healing brew first."

"Yes, ma'am."

She laughed. "Quit saying that!"

"I'm just trying to be a model patient. What's next? Do you give me an alcohol rub all over my fever-racked body?"

"No!"

"Some doctor you are."

"Aspirin," she said, getting to her feet. "That's what you need."

Mitch dutifully swallowed his pills, finished the lemonade, and followed Chelsey into the bedroom.

She pulled back the blankets on the bed. "Climb in there," she said.

"Alone?"

"Mitch!"

"Okay, okay," he said, reaching for the belt on his pants.

"What are you doing?"

"Going to bed like you told me to!"

"But last time you slept in your jeans."

"Dress slacks aren't that comfortable, Chelsey. I need proper rest, right?"

"Yes, I—I guess so. Well, hurry it up."

Mitch chuckled softly as he pulled off his socks and dropped his pants to the floor. He shrugged out of his shirt, leaving him clad only in royal blue briefs.

"I'd better fold this stuff up," he said.

"I'll do it! You just get under those covers."

"Yes, ma'am," he said, which was rewarded by a snort of disgust by Chelsey. "You shouldn't play doctor in your fancy dress," he said, lying down and pulling the sheet up only to his waist. "You'll mess it up during brain surgery."

"I suppose you think I should put on my Dr. Denton's?"

"Nope." He produced the sheer nightie from beneath her pillow. "This will do nicely."

Chelsey snatched the filmy material from him and stuffed it in her dresser drawer, replacing it with a faded football jersey. She marched into the bathroom to change and when she returned, Mitch had his arm thrown over his eyes and his breathing was steady and even. Chelsey hung up her dress, banned Myrtle to the sofa, and carefully folded Mitch's clothes and placed them on a chair. Finally she slid into bed next to him and shut off the light.

Just how high was his fever? she wondered, moving closer and peering at him. He was sleeping peacefully, which was a good sign. Lord, he was gorgeous, with the moonlight flickering over his face and glistening chest. He was sick as a dog and was still beautiful. Why didn't he just quit messing around and fall madly in love with her?

Mitch moaned softly and Chelsey scrambled to her knees and leaned over his massive frame. Suddenly strong hands gripped her shoulders and she yelped in surprise as Mitch flung her back against the pillow and covered her body with his.

"You were faking!" she said.

"I was waiting to see if you were going to give me a thorough examination, doc."

"You're despicable!"

"Now that is a great word."

"Mitch, get off me and go to sleep!"

"Yes, ma'am. In a minute, ma'am." He slowly lowered his head to claim her mouth in a fiery kiss that set off sparklers of desire through Chelsey's body.

Mitch lifted his head and gasped, and then a rumble of laughter escaped from his throat.

"Whatever is your problem?" she asked.

"I can't breathe when I kiss you," he said, grinning. "My air passages are clogged or something. You're going to have a hard time explaining to the cops how I died."

"Then stop kissing me!"

"I don't want to." He placed a nibbling ribbon of kisses down her throat. "It's a helluva nice way to cash in my chips."

"Mitch, for Pete's sake, you are—oh!" She cried out as his hand slid along her thigh.

"So soft," he murmured, seeking her mouth once again, his questing tongue brought a muffled moan from Chelsey. "Dammit," he roared, flopping back onto his pillow, "I'm suffocating! I haven't seen my lady in nearly a week and I can't even kiss her! I'm going to sue my father for sending me to San Francisco! Take him to court! Do you hear me?"

"Mitch, calm down," Chelsey said, mentally giving the same directive to the desire that was raging within her.

"Well, dammit to hell!"

"Quit swearing! That isn't going to help. You really are a lousy patient."

"I know what we can do, doc. We'll study anatomy by Braille."

"Mitchell Michael, shut up!"

"Oh-h-h, I feel rotten." He groaned. "I'm going to have to die to get better."

"You have three seconds to clam up or I'm going on the sofa with Myrtle."

"Would you really do that?"

"Yep," she said, folding her arms over her breasts.

"You are not a kind person, Chelsey, but I'm crazy about you anyway."

"You're crazy all right. Be quiet."

"Yes, ma'am."

"Cripes," she said, punching her pillow and flopping over onto her stomach.

A silence fell over the room and Chelsey felt herself beginning to drift off to sleep.

"Chelsey?"

"What!" she shrieked.

"Good night."

"Good night, Mitch," she said, laughing softly.

Chelsey awoke in the middle of the night and gently placed her hand on Mitch's forehead. A rush of relief swept over her at the feel of his cool skin. She wasn't such a crummy doctor after all, she decided smugly. Mitch's fever had broken and his breathing was less congested. He could probably even kiss her without passing out from lack of oxygen. She carefully slid to his side of the bed and snuggled next to him, her head resting on his shoulder. Zork's snoring was the only sound in the room that was aglow with moonlight, and a serene sense of contentment brought a smile to Chelsey's lips.

For better, for worse, she thought dreamily. In sickness and in health. Forsaking the world if need be, that was how deeply she loved Mitch Brannon. But would he ever come to love her as she did him?

"Oh, Mitch," Chelsey sighed.

"Hmmm?" he said foggily.

"Nothing, nothing. Go back to sleep."

"Yes . . . ma'am," he mumbled.

The next morning, Chelsey managed to crawl off the bed without waking Mitch and dressed in shorts and a T-shirt. As she walked through the living room she jumped in surprise as Polly's whispering voice came out of the box on the wall.

"Chelsey?"

"Hi, Polly. Why are you whispering?"

"I know Mitch is back in town and his truck is still at your house and I didn't want to disturb you if you were . . . you know."

"We're playing doctor," Chelsey said merrily.

"Really? I suppose that could be just as much fun."

"No, dope. Mitch caught a very bad cold and I'm fixing him up."

"Oh. Well, give him hot lemonade."

"I know that! Everything all right at Annie's house?"

"Yes, I came over to water the plants. Chelsey, was Mitch glad to see you, just overjoyed and stuff?"

"I would say so, yes."

"Hey, maybe I was wrong about what I said about him getting ready to split the scene."

Chelsey frowned. "But maybe you were right."

"How are you going to find out what he's up to?"

"All I can do is wait and see. I can't exactly ask him, you know."

"No, I guess not. Isn't it a little tough on the nerves?"

"Very."

"I hope we don't end up hating Mitch, Chelsey, 'cause he's such a super guy. I think. Isn't he?"

"Go water the plants, Polly."

"Okay. 'Bye. I mean, over and out."

Chelsey ate a breakfast of fresh fruit, toast, and coffee, then made a tray of a matching menu and carried it into the bedroom.

"Mitch?" she called softly. "Mitch?"

"Go away, Mike. You snored all night again," he mumbled.

"That was Zork. Would you like some food?"

"Huh?" he said, opening his eyes. "Oh, hi, babe. Say, is this service with a smile? Classy place."

"Of course. How are you feeling?"

"I don't know yet," he said, pushing himself up to a

sitting position and placing the tray on his lap. "I'll tell you when I wake up."

"You look good," she said, her gaze sweeping over his broad chest and down to the sheet that just covered the waistband of his briefs. "Excellent, in fact."

"I need a shave. I really thank you for taking such fine care of me . . . ma'am." He smiled. "I do believe I'm going to live."

"The female population of San Diego will be relieved to hear that."

"I have one woman, Chelsey Star. You."

"That's nice," she said softly, sitting down on the edge of the bed.

"Hey, why the frown? You didn't catch my cold, did you?"

"No, I'm fine. I'm so glad you're better."

"Chelsey, is something wrong? You're acting as though you're very preoccupied. Do you, or we, have a problem?"

"I don't know, Mitch. Do we?"

Damn, why had she spoken to Polly? she thought. Now all the questions, the doubts were whirling through her mind. She had to push them away, keep them at bay before they consumed her.

"I've been a very happy man since I met you, Chelsey," Mitch said seriously, looking directly into her eyes. "You brought sunshine into my life and made me smile. I cherish you, Chelsey. I really do."

For how long? her mind screamed. Cherish? Dammit, why couldn't he *love* her? "There's no problem, Mitch," she said. "Want some hot lemonade?"

"Lord, no! You nearly did me in with that lethal brew. These are delicious bananas. Did you make them yourself? You know, when you weren't busy baking bread?"

"Certainly, and the coffee beans too."

He nodded. "You're a talented lady. You can pick from a multitude of choices for your future career."

"Dammit," Chelsey snapped, getting to her feet, "would you quit harping about my future?"

"Lord, Chelsey! Hey, babe, what is it? What's wrong?"

"Mitch, I—I—"

"Talk to me!"

"Mitch, I want you to make love to me! Right now! This—this very minute!"

Eight

"Could you run that by me a little slower?" Mitch said, a deep frown on his face.

"You heard me! Take off your clothes!" Chelsey yelled.

"I hardly have any on!"

"Good. That'll save time!"

"Chelsey, what in the hell is going on?" Mitch bellowed. "One minute we're talking about coffee beans and the next thing I know you're— Have you been sniffing glue or something? You can't just suddenly decide to—"

"Oh, yeah? Watch me!" she said, reaching for the zipper on her shorts.

"Don't touch that! Now, babe, calm down. I don't know what's set you off here, but we'll discuss it thoroughly and get it all squared away and—"

"Don't you want to make love to me, Mitch Brannon?"

"Of course I do! You know that."

"So do it, dammit!"

" 'Do it, dammit'?" He grinned. "Are you sure it isn't, 'So, dammit, do it'?"

"Are you laughing at me? If you are, I swear I'm going to break your nose," she said, bursting into tears.

"Oh, Lord, now you're crying. I don't understand any of this," he said, throwing up his hands.

"Well, I don't understand one thing you're doing either, so we're even. I can't take any more of this!"

"Any more of what?" he asked, setting the tray on the floor and getting out of the bed.

"How dare you stand there practically naked!"

"You just told me to take my clothes off!"

"Get back in that bed!"

"Sweet heaven," he muttered, flopping down and yanking the sheet up. "Now tell me what it is you can't take any more of."

"Your loans and furniture and artichoke hearts," she said, sniffling.

"Huh?"

"And my future! My damnable future!"

"What? Can't you stop crying? You're not making any sense. Artichoke hearts?"

"Yes! Why are you doing all of this? What is it you're trying to tell me? I don't want to believe Polly is right, but . . ."

"What has Polly got to do with anything?"

"She really likes you, but she's just calling it as she sees it."

"What have I done wrong?" Mitch yelled.

"Nothing! Or maybe everything! I don't know!"

"Chelsey, for heaven's sake, would you slow down and explain this? Do you want to start with the artichoke hearts?"

"Yes, and—oh, hell, there's someone at the door."

Chelsey brushed the tears off her cheeks as she stalked to the front door and flung it open.

"Richard!" she gasped. "What are you doing here?"

"I want to talk to you," he growled, hobbling into the room on his crutches. "I got a ride down with a friend of mine. You and I are going to have a serious discussion, Chelsey."

"Oh, Lord," she said, wringing her hands as she glanced quickly at the bedroom door.

"Have you been crying?" Richard yelled.

"Richard, please be quiet," she said.

"Who am I disturbing? Zork? Myrtle's deaf, remember? Unless . . . Whose truck is that outside?"

"Chelsey?" Mitch said, coming into the room.

"Oh, thank goodness," she whispered. "He put his pants on."

"Who in the hell is this?" Richard roared.

"I might ask you the same question, buddy," Mitch said, crossing his arms over his bare chest.

"The name is Star. Richard Star."

"Oops," Mitch said. "Brother Richard. You didn't tell me he was a mountain, Chelsey. Which six positions on the football team did you play, Rich?"

"It's Richard . . . buddy," he said, "and I'm still waiting to hear who you are and what you were doing in my sister's bed!"

"It's none of your business," Chelsey said. "I am the big sister and you are the little brother."

"When it comes to this stuff, I'm no *little* brother! I'm going to take this guy apart."

"I never hit cripples," Mitch said, grinning. "You're a member of the walking wounded, Star. I'll be glad to give you a raincheck, though. By the way, I'm Mitch Brannon."

"Outside, Brannon," Richard said, gesturing to the door with his crutch. "We're settling this right now!"

"Whatever you say." Mitch shrugged and started across the room.

"Hold it! I said, hold it!" Chelsey shrieked. "Would you two just knock it off?"

"That's exactly what I intend to do," Richard said. "Outside, Brannon."

"Could we make up our minds here?" Mitch asked.

"That's it!" Chelsey said, planting her hands on her hips. "I've had it! Sit down!"

"Okay," Mitch said, sinking onto the sofa. "I really didn't want to mess up your baby brother's face. He's so cute, ya know?"

"I'm going to kill him!" Richard said.

"Don't push me, Star," Mitch said, shaking his head. "You don't know what you're talking about anyway. I haven't slept with Chelsey."

"That's none of his business!" Chelsey said angrily.

"Yes, it is," Mitch said. "If you were my sister, I'd beat me to a pulp. Did that make sense? Look, Richard, I know it looks bad, but nothing happened here. I had a rotten cold and Chelsey was taking care of me."

"Lord, did she make you drink hot lemonade?"

"Yeah. Cripes, I nearly croaked."

"Never tell her when you're sick. No matter what's wrong, she'll give you that damn hot lemonade. Even when I had the measles she—"

"I am going to murder you both!" Chelsey screamed at the top of her lungs. "You are giving me the crazies!"

"You don't have to come unglued, Chelsey," Richard said, lowering himself onto the rocker and placing his crutches on the floor. "If Mitch says nothing happened then—"

"So who is he? Your best friend?" she snapped. "Exactly why are you here, Richard?"

"It has to do with the check you sent me. We agreed there would be no loans and then you up and get one. And where did this new furniture come from? Did you cut your hair? About the money, Chelsey . . ."

"I loaned it to her," Mitch said. "Interest free. Richard, she was working overtime and, Lord, man, she fainted from exhaustion right into my arms. I had to do something. Chelsey is very important to me and it was blowing my mind to see what she was doing."

"It's my fault," Richard said. "If I hadn't busted my ankle . . . I'll pay it back, Brannon. Every penny."

"Don't worry about it. Everything is under control here now."

Richard nodded. "I can see that."

"Are you two finished discussing me as if I wasn't in the room?" Chelsey asked.

"Isn't she adorable, Richard?" Mitch said, laughing. "I'm telling you, she's just the cutest thing. Really keeps a guy on his toes 'cause she's so damn unpredictable. I loaned her my truck and old lead foot here got a speeding ticket."

"Oh, shut up," Chelsey said, bursting into tears again.

"Uh-oh," Mitch said, getting to his feet.

"I think we're in trouble," Richard said.

"Chelsey!" Polly yelled from the porch. "Can I come in?"

"Why can't she just knock like normal people?" Mitch said. "Enter, Polly. Chelsey, don't cry. I'm sorry if we upset you."

"Don't speak to me," Chelsey said as Mitch pulled her close to his chest and rested his chin on the top of her head.

"Hi, everybody!" Polly said cheerfully. "Hey, racy Richard, good to see you. Why is Chelsey crying? Did something happen to Zork or Myrtle?"

"Everything is fine, Polly," Richard said. "It was all a misunderstanding."

"Oh?" Polly said. "Because Mitch is half naked?"

"No, I am not," Mitch said indignantly. "I'm half dressed."

"You've got a point there." Polly nodded. "You're better-looking every time I see you, Richard. I adore red-haired men. Want to marry me?"

"I would, but I'm already engaged."

"Oh, that's right. I forgot."

"I will take you to lunch, though, if you'll drive. I've caused enough flack around here."

"You're on."

"Could you drop me over on Mission Bay later? I have to connect with my ride."

"Sure."

"Chelsey," Richard said, "I'm sorry about the way I came charging in here."

"That's all right," she said, not budging from Mitch's arms. "Please take good care of yourself."

"I will. Brannon," he said, extending his hand, "you're a good man. Thanks for everything. Look after our Chelsey, okay?"

"You bet," Mitch said, shaking Richard's hand.

"Whew!" Richard flexed his fingers. "I'm glad we didn't go outside. I'd be a dead body by now."

"You were going to take on Muscles Mitchell?" Polly said. "Richard, you are stupid."

Richard laughed. "Seemed like a good idea at the time. 'Bye, y'all."

" 'Bye, dum-dum," Chelsey muttered.

A silence fell over the small room after Polly and Richard left, and Chelsey drew a long, shuddering breath.

"Nope, it's never dull around here," Mitch finally said, still holding her tightly in his arms. "Could we sit down now?"

"Yes," she said. She snuggled next to him as they sat down on the sofa.

"We're going to back up to just after the coffee beans. What happened, Chelsey?"

"I freaked out."

"That sums it up pretty well. Would you care to elaborate?"

"No."

"Chelsey, you were terribly upset and it was obviously caused by something I've done. I think we should talk about it."

"No."

"Oh, man," he said, shaking his head, "this isn't good. We're supposed to work through our problems, communicate, discuss them. Please tell me what I did wrong about—about the artichoke hearts."

"Oh, Mitch." Chelsey laughed. "When you put it like that I feel ridiculous. I'm sorry I caused such a scene. Couldn't we just forget the whole thing?"

"I don't think that's a good idea. You were crying! Crying, Chelsey."

"That's a privilege of my gender."

"It rips me up."

"No, that's what Richard was going to do."

"I like your brother. I wouldn't have acted differently in his place. Lord, the guy thought I was sleeping with his sister!"

"Which is none of his business."

"So you said several times. Speaking of that, would you mind explaining why you suddenly ordered me to ravish your body?"

"I did not! Well, I sort of did. No, you're right. I did."

"And?"

"Oh, Mitch, I don't know. Everything just piled up on me all of a sudden. I didn't want to think about my future, the tomorrows and what they might bring. There was only the moment and I wanted you. I realize I wasn't very ladylike about it, but I meant it. You're the only man I have ever offered myself to. I want to experience lovemaking with you, Mitch, and I would never regret my actions. Never."

"Chelsey, you're making it so difficult for me. I can't perform for you so you can find out what it's all about. It's too important, too special for someone like you. If I were just another in a string of men, that'd be different. But to be the first . . . Chelsey, I have feelings too. You'd be using me to satisfy a certain curiosity about something you don't know anything about. It's because I care so deeply for you that I can't do it. I just can't."

"Why? Because you think I'm waiting for my Prince Charming?"

"Well, yes. You said—"

"Mitch, I've grown up about that. There aren't any more Prince Charmings left."

"Sure there are."

"No. Cinderella snatched up the last one. Besides, it's too late for me anyway."

"What do you mean?"

"I blew it. You see, Mitch, I—I fell in love with you. I didn't intend to tell you but I'm rather irrational today. I wasn't going to flip out over the artichoke hearts either, but I did. That's it in a nutshell. I love you, Mitchell Michael Brannon. How's that for royally messing up our relationship?"

"You . . . love me?"

"Yes, I do."

"Love me? Are in love with me?"

"Aren't you paying attention?" she yelled.

"Yes, of course, I heard you. I—man, this is overwhelming. I don't suppose you could forget about it for a while? I mean, put it on hold until—no, that's dumb. You jumped the gun on me here. You were supposed to—dammit, now what am I going to do?"

"Why are you babbling? I'm sure I'm not the first woman to fall in love with you."

"No, but—"

"I knew it!"

"You don't understand. I had this all worked out."

"What are you talking about?"

"Nothing, nothing," Mitch said, getting to his feet and pacing the floor. "I've got to think this through."

"Just tell me you don't want to see me again and get it over with," Chelsey said, staring at her hands, which were clutched tightly in her lap.

"Why in the hell would I do that?"

"Because I gummed it up."

"I never said that! You just surprised me, that's all. Are you absolutely sure you love me?"

"Positive."

"Yeah, I can see it in your eyes when you say it. Okay, I'll—uh—regroup and . . . I have to go home now, Chelsey."

"What?"

"Yes, that's what I have to do," he said, heading for the bedroom.

"Whatever." She shrugged. "I'm perfectly capable of having a nervous breakdown alone."

"I'll pick you up at six o'clock," Mitch said a few moments later as he came into the room buttoning his shirt.

"What for?"

"Dinner. Dress casually, jeans or something."

"But . . ."

"See ya," he said, walking to the door.

"You didn't even kiss me good-bye," she wailed.

"Lord, I forgot. You really boggled my mind." He hurried back and gave her a quick peck. "There. Good-bye."

"Oh, wonderful." Chelsey moaned as the truck roared out of the driveway. "I have such a big mouth. Why in hell's bells did I tell him I love him? Zork! We're going bike riding."

Chelsey rode until she was exhausted and Zork's tongue was hanging out. He collapsed on the floor and fell asleep before Chelsey could even take off his candy apple red sunglasses. She then showered and shampooed her hair and set a batch of bread to rise.

What she did not do was think. She simply blanked her mind and went about her business, refusing to dwell on the disastrous state of her existence. She chatted with Annie on the telephone, worked in the garden, baked the bread, and then decided to take another shower. Dressed in jeans and a bright yellow blouse she sat on the sofa and waited for Mitch to arrive.

"Hello," he said when she answered his knock at six. "May I come in?"

"Of course," she said, eying him warily. "Why would you ask?"

"Just checking." He entered the living room and pulled her into his arms. "Don't want to make any more mistakes."

"Oh, I see. Well—" Chelsey's words were silenced by his lips claiming hers in a kiss that went on and on and on. His hands slid down over her firm buttocks and pressed her against the hard planes of his body.

She was dizzy when he finally released her and had to grip his arm for support as she took a steadying breath. Just as she decided she wasn't going to pass out, he kissed her again with a vehemence that caused a moan to escape from her throat. She molded herself against him, returning the kiss wholeheartedly as his hands moved over her back and to the sides of her breasts. The evidence of Mitch's arousal pressed against her and Chelsey relished its announcement of need, rejoiced in the desire that was consuming them both.

"Ready to leave?" he asked finally, taking a ragged breath and wiping a line of perspiration from his brow.

"Where are we going?" she asked dreamily.

"Dinner, remember?"

"I'm not hungry."

"Come on," he said, taking her by the hand. "They're expecting us."

"They who?"

"My parents."

"We're having dinner with your parents?" she exclaimed.

"Yes."

"Then why are we wearing jeans? I mean, shouldn't I dress up more?"

"No, my father is barbecuing outside. Let's go."

"Mitch, was there some special significance behind the fact that you just kissed the living daylights out of me?"

"Yes! No! I enjoy kissing you, that's all. You're a very kissable person."

"Oh."

The senior Brannon's ranch-style home was even larger than Mitch's and boasted a sparkling swimming pool in the midst of the perfectly manicured backyard. There was also a swing set which Mitch explained was for Mike's daughters and white wrought-iron tables and chairs.

"Hello!" Frank Brannon called from his spot in front of a brick barbecue.

"Hi." Mitch waved.

"Right on time," Kathleen Brannon said, coming across the grass with a tray. "Daiquiris for everyone. How's your cold, Mitch?"

"I'm cured."

"That's good. I read in a magazine just the other day that the best thing for a cold is hot lemonade. I never knew that when I was raising you boys."

"Praise the Lord," Mitch mumbled.

"It's lovely to see you again, Chelsey," Kathleen said. "Let's sit down. Frank will join us when he's all organized over there. Mike and his crew couldn't come, Mitch. They had other plans. He said to give him more of a warning next time when you wanted to get together."

"I'm sick of looking at him anyway," Mitch said. "I wanted Chelsey to meet Rachel and the girls."

"Well, we'll all plan something for another time," Kathleen said as they settled on the chairs under a large shady tree.

"You have a lovely home, Mrs. Brannon," Chelsey said.

"Thank you, dear, but do call me Kathleen. The house is a bit large for Frank and me now but I refuse to move. Our granddaughters like to spend the night and, well, I raised my children here. There are just too many memories within those walls to ever leave."

"I think that's very nice." Chelsey smiled. "I'm sure I'd feel the same way."

"Then you're unusual," Kathleen said. "So many young women today place their careers above motherhood and the family. Those that do choose to stay home and raise their children sometimes find themselves defending their beliefs. It would require a great deal of fortitude."

"That's right!" Mitch said, punching his fist in the air and causing Chelsey to jump in surprise. "That woman would have to be very in touch with herself. Know what I mean? Once those little baby buggers start coming along you can't ship them back to the factory. Yes, sir! That gal would have to be very sure she knew what she was doing, had explored all the other avenues open to her before she made that choice."

"Who put a nickel in you?" Chelsey said, looking at him with wide eyes.

He shrugged. "I'm merely expressing my opinion. It's a free country."

"And you have a valid point, Mitch," Kathleen said. "Some girls jump into marriage and babies before they've had a chance to grow within themselves and satisfy their personal needs. Then later they become restless, bored, feel they were cheated out of a slice of life. It's very sad."

"Very," Mitch said, shaking his head.

"That's all very true," Chelsey said, "but there are some who know, who have always known, what their values are, what it will take to make them truly happy. Not everyone goes through identity crises these days."

"I certainly never did," Kathleen said. "We didn't even have that term in my day, but it was a less complicated era, I suppose."

"The role of wife and mother is an ancient institution," Mitch boomed. "It shall not be diminished by the rigors of time!"

"Hear, hear," Frank Brannon said, joining the group. "What's the topic of your next sermon, Mitch?"

"Fatherhood. You flunked."

"Kathleen, tell your son to knock off his tantrum because I sent him to San Francisco. He's getting on my nerves."

"I do apologize, sir," Mitch said, shaking his father's hand. "By the way, be sure and mark my next birthday on your calendar. It's going to be a splendid event, a happening, a peak experience."

"I'm ignoring you, Mitch," Frank said. "So how are you, Chelsey? And your dog and cat?"

"We're all fine, thanks," she said.

"Mitch tells me you work in computers," Frank said, sitting down and sipping his drink, "but that you find it a bit dull."

"Well, I . . . yes, I do," Chelsey said. "I can't deny that. I think it's because they're so . . . inhuman."

"You'd prefer dealing with people?" Frank asked pleasantly.

"I've never given it much thought. I haven't been in a position to switch careers anyway."

"Until now," Mitch said quietly.

"With your skills, you could teach others to operate the machines," Frank said. "Wouldn't that bring a human quality into it?"

"I suppose so, yes."

"Think about it," Frank said, peering at her over the rim of his glass.

"When do we eat?" Mitch asked. "I'm starving. Are we having potatoes?"

"Of course, dear," Kathleen said. "I wouldn't dream of serving you a meal without them."

"At Chelsey's I get them home-grown," Mitch said smugly.

"How marvelous." Kathleen beamed.

Nice, maybe, Chelsey thought, shaking her head slightly, but Buster's potatoes were hardly marvelous. Were these people actually getting excited about potatoes?

"By the way, Mitch," Kathleen went on, "don't threaten to shoot your brother anymore. It's just not socially acceptable behavior."

"He had it coming," Mitch said. "Besides, it was a squirt gun. He never gives you all the facts. Remember the time when I was fourteen and he said I hot-wired the truck and went joyriding? Well, that simply wasn't true."

"Oh?" Frank said, raising his eyebrows.

"Nope. I stole the keys out of your pants pocket and *then* went joyriding. See? Mike screws up everything he says."

"Oh, my." Chelsey laughed.

"Don't confess anything else," Frank said, chuckling. "I'm too old for this."

It had been, Chelsey decided when she and Mitch returned to her house, an exhausting evening. The conversation changed topics so fast that she had hardly been able to keep up. Somewhere in the middle of things she had exchanged recipes with Kathleen for bread and brownies, and then, for Pete's sake, they were all debating the subject of breast-feeding babies in public places.

The topper had been when a beautiful blond woman had swooped into the yard with two little girls in tow who were dressed in their pajamas. She had turned out to be Mike's wife Rachel and had muttered something about being afraid she'd be too late, then instructed the girls to kiss their grandparents and uncle good night. Did people actually lug their kids across town for a smooch before bedtime? Chelsey had wondered. Brannons did. They were all a bunch of nutsy-cuckoos. Nice, but definitely loony-tunes.

"Did you enjoy yourself?" Mitch asked as he sat down on the sofa.

"Oh, yes, very much. Your family is . . . interesting. They made me feel very welcome."

"That's good. Plant your cute tush here," he said, patting the cushion next to him.

"Why?"

"Because I'm going to kiss you for a while."

"How long?"

"Oh, a day or two give or take a day or two."

"Huh?"

"Come here."

"Okay, sounds reasonable to me."

Due to the fact that strong hands grabbed her around the waist and redirected her descent, Chelsey's cute tush landed on Mitch's lap and her mouth was instantly covered by his. His fingers moved to the buttons on her blouse and as the kiss intensified, he deftly removed the garment and dropped it on the floor. Her bra followed close behind.

Chelsey gasped as he leaned her back in his arms and drew the rosy nipple of one breast into his mouth, flickering the bud into pulsating tautness with his tongue.

"Mitch . . ."

"So soft," he murmured, "so beautiful. Unbutton my shirt, Chelsey. Touch me, please."

With trembling hands she complied, trailing her fingers through the curly tawny chest hair. She could feel his muscles tense under her foray as she found and stroked his nipples. He kissed her roughly, then with seductive gentleness, his lips and tongue dancing over her face, throat, her full breasts, to the flat plane of her stomach.

"Oh, Mitch," Chelsey moaned as desire surged through her, causing her to arch her body against him and feel the pressure of his aroused manhood.

"Say it again," he said, his voice strained. "Tell me you love me. I have to know, Chelsey."

"I do love you, Mitch. I love you so very much."

"I want to make love to you. Tonight, Chelsey. Now. If you're going to stop me, do it before it's too late."

Oh, Lord! Chelsey thought. He meant it! This was it! She had about three seconds to make a decision that would affect the rest of her life! But there was no decision to make. She loved this man, this Mitchell Michael Brannon, and always would. She would come to him willingly, in absolute honesty and trust, and never regret having shared with him the greatest gift between man and woman. He was her Prince Charming and she would hold him in her loving embrace for as long as he chose to stay.

"Love me, Mitch," she whispered. "I've waited a lifetime for you."

"You won't be sorry?"

"No, never. I promise you, Mitch, there will be no tears."

"It'll be beautiful. Beautiful, Chelsey. But, listen to me. The first time, it's going to hurt you. I'm sorry, but that's how it is, but after that, we'll have the whole night."

"Yes," she said, placing her hand on his cheek.

Mitch pushed himself to his feet with Chelsey held tightly against his chest and carried her into the bedroom. He kicked the door shut with his foot, leaving a confused Zork and Myrtle staring at the wooden barrier that blocked their entrance.

He laid Chelsey on the bed and sat down next to her, placing one large hand on each side of her head as he kissed her. She slid her hands over his chest, then down to the waistband of his jeans, the motion causing him to lift his head slightly and take a sharp breath. Their eyes met and held, each reading the message of desire in the other's. Then Mitch unzipped her jeans and drew them down her slender legs with her bikini panties.

As she lay before him naked, Chelsey sighed and smiled. A sudden wave of peace and contentment swept over her. Yes, it was time, but only because the man was her beloved Mitch. Her doubts and fears were all erased by the smoldering depth of his tender gaze, the touch of his hands and lips and body, his aura of strength and beauty. He was hers.

"You're even more lovely than I'd imagined," Mitch said, his voice raspy. "I've dreamed of this moment, ached with wanting you."

His eyes never leaving hers, Mitch stood and shrugged out of his clothes. He stood perfectly still as Chelsey studied his magnificent form, her eyes roaming over his perfectly proportioned body, the thrusting announcement of his manhood.

"Are you frightened, Chelsey?" he asked softly.

She didn't speak; she simply raised her arms to welcome him back into her embrace. He stretched out next to her, the heat from his rugged body seeming like the comforting warmth of the sun. Slowly, languorously, he caressed and kissed all of her soft body, bringing her to a fever pitch of desire. His hand slid to the inner flesh of her thigh and on to the core of her femininity, and Chelsey gasped and dug her fingers into his arm.

"Oh, Mitch, please," she whispered.

"Soon, babe," he said, his mouth finding the rosy bud of one throbbing breast.

"Mitch!"

"Yes, Chelsey." He moved away for a moment, reached in the pocket of his jeans, and quickly prepared himself. He covered her body with his then, parting her legs with his knee and gazing down into her passion-flushed face. "Hold on to me. The pain will only last a moment. Just hold on tight."

And then he was there. With a thrust, he won the victory over nature's barrier and gritted his teeth as Chelsey cried out from the hot flash of pain. Then slowly, slowly he began to move within her, watching the wonder, the rapture that crossed her face. With instincts as ancient as womankind itself, Chelsey's femininity awakened, spread its soft petals, and responded in perfect rhythm to the motions of Mitch's body. She arched her back to draw him further within her, to allow his manhood to consume and fill her.

They soared together, higher and higher until suddenly in a burst of strange and glorious dancing colors Chelsey exploded into ecstasy.

"Mitch!" she gasped, clutching his shoulders. "Oh, Mitch!"

"Yes," he said, and then shuddered above her as he joined her. He collapsed against her with a ragged sigh, then pushed himself up to rest on his arms, his eyes darting over her face. "Chelsey?"

"Hmmm?" she said dreamily, smiling at him crookedly.

"Chelsey?"

"Yes?"

"Talk to me! Say you're all right. Say I didn't hurt you. Say it was as beautiful for you as it was for me. It was, wasn't it? Chelsey?"

"It was . . . incredible. Oh, Mitch, I feel absolutely wonderful, divine, fantastic. Is it always like that or was that a fluke?"

He grinned. "It gets even better."

"Really?"

"Really," he said, lowering his head to find her lips.

Really! Chelsey thought much later as she snuggled close to Mitch. He had aroused her with a single kiss, sent her desires soaring as his manhood stirred within her, telling of his rekindled passion. Their journey of delight had been beyond description in its splendor and Chelsey vowed to remember every moment of this time she had shared with the man she loved.

"Chelsey," Mitch said, brushing her damp hair from her forehead, "I'm so sorry I had to hurt you like that."

"I've already forgotten it. Mitch, this has been the most beautiful night of my life. I love you so much."

"And I—Chelsey, there aren't words to tell you. . . ."

Honored? No, that's no good. Humble? Grateful? Hell, I can't explain what it meant to have you choose me to give your most precious gift to."

"I think I understand. Thank you for being such a good lover."

"Oh?" He chuckled, the sound rich and throaty. "And how do you know I am?"

"Well, aren't you?"

"So I've been told, yes. The phrases 'terrific' and 'magnificent' have been tossed around a bit here and there too."

"Shut up, Mitch."

"Right."

"We didn't get ourselves pregnant, did we?"

"I took care of it. You were such a space case already, I guess you missed that little transaction. Chelsey, you were wonderful. You gave of yourself so completely. I can't believe how much trust you put in me!"

"If you can't trust Mitch Brannon, who can you trust?"

"Oh, man, you are crazy!" Mitch laughed. "Hey, what's that noise?"

"That, sir, is your pal Zork, whining outside the door that you slammed in his face."

"Poor guy," Mitch said, swinging his feet to the floor and walking across the room.

"You've got a great body, Brannon," Chelsey said as Zork came bounding into the room.

"And it's all yours," he said, stretching out next to her again. "And, Chelsey Star, you are all mine. Mine, Chelsey."

"I know," she said softly. Forever, she thought. She wasn't sorry she'd given herself to Mitch, but if only he loved her. Well, she couldn't have everything and at least for now he was there. Scarlett O'Hara got away with worrying about everything tomorrow and so could Chelsey. Tonight was hers and Mitch's. The future be damned.

"Chelsey, I know it's not very practical for me to stay here on a Sunday, but I don't want to leave you alone. I'll drive you to work in the morning. Just humor me on this. I have this inner fear that if I go home you'll start thinking about what we did and be sorry it happened."

"No, I wouldn't!"

"Let me stay, all right?"

"Yes, of course. I want you to."

"Would you like to explain about the artichoke hearts yet?"

"No!" She laughed. "I would not!"

"I really hate it when you cry," he said, pulling her close. "It makes my heart hurt. It does! I get a sharp pain in my ticker. I don't ever want to be the cause of your tears again."

For a smart man, Mitch sure was dumb, Chelsey thought. What did she expect her to do when he disappeared from her life, throw a party? And he *would* go. Oh, it just didn't make sense! They had shared so much, come so far, why couldn't he take that final step and commit himself to a lifetime of happiness with her?

"Go to sleep, Chelsey," Mitch whispered.

"Good night, Mitch. I'm glad you're here."

"There's no place else I want to be, Chelsey mine. See you in the morning, Cinderella."

Cinderella? she thought sleepily. If only it were true. Then she could keep her Prince Charming.

"Chelsey?"

"Yes, Mitch?"

"Tell me once more that you love me, okay? Then I promise I'll be quiet."

"I love you, Mitch. I love you very much."

"Thanks," he said softly. "It's not a big enough word, but it's the only one I can come up with. Tonight was . . . special."

"I'll never forget it," she said. "Not ever."

Nine

"Look deep into my eyes," Chelsey said, her voice low and dramatic.

"Okay," Mitch said, leaning across the table and pressing his nose onto hers. "Now what?"

"Do I appear different? I mean, is everyone at work going to say, 'Ah-ha! That girl has been made love to. Not once but three, count them, three times'?"

"No, my sweet." He laughed. "It's our secret. And Zork's. I forgot he was asleep on the floor this morning when we . . . you know. I don't like him in the room when I make love to you. It's kinky."

"He's my dog, not my son!"

"He doesn't know that. Ask him. He'll tell you he's going to kindergarten in a couple of years."

"I'll buy him a lunch box with matching sunglasses and new crayons."

"Eat your grapes."

"Right."

"Chelsey, you were so wonderful last night," Mitch

164

said quietly. "And this morning. Is everything all right? I mean, you're not sorry?"

"No, Mitch, I'm not sorry and I never will be. What we shared was ours alone and it was an incredibly beautiful time in my life. I'm very glad I waited for you, Mitch."

"Oh, Chelsey mine, you make me feel like a million bucks. I—I am a lucky man."

In the parking lot of the computer company, Mitch pulled Chelsey across the seat of the truck and kissed her so passionately she forgot where she was.

"Work?" she mumbled when Mitch said she was going to be late.

He chuckled. "In that building, remember?"

"Got it."

"Want to go visit Annie tonight?"

"Oh, yes, she'd love seeing you, Golden Boy."

"Okay, I'll pick you up about seven. 'Bye, babe."

Chelsey slid out of the cab, waved good-bye, and then hollered at Tony to wait for her.

"Don't come near me," Tony said out of the corner of his mouth. "Brannon hasn't left the parking lot yet."

"Good grief," Chelsey said, falling in step beside him.

"Want me to take your pulse, Chels?"

"Huh?"

"I saw that kiss. Hot stuff. I could go for a dose of that for breakfast."

"It's better than oatmeal, kid."

"Isn't it kind of early for a date? Or are you running a little late from last night's. Or—"

"Mind your own business."

"You're right. I'm sorry. Is he in love with you yet, Chels?"

"Mind your own business."

"Wrong answer. If he was, you'd be tripping over your tongue to tell me. Chelsey, why are you staying in a relationship that's going to break your heart?"

"I love him, Tony. I can't change how I feel."

"But he doesn't love *you*. Dammit, he's got to be crazy. Did all that muscle spread to his brain?"

"Don't make me sad today, Tony. Not today."

"Okay, Chels." He sighed. "I'll back off. I'm here if you need me."

"Thanks, my friend. How's the flight attendant?"

"She dumped me for a pilot. Guys in uniform have an unfair advantage."

"You could join the army."

"They'd cut my sexy hair. Besides, I've got a date tonight with a cute little nurse I met when I visited Annie at the hospital. Annie wants me to drop by first so she can give me a few tips on how to make this girl putty in my hands."

"And?"

"Do I look stupid? I'm seeing Annie on my lunch hour."

"Oh, my." Chelsey laughed.

When she sat down in front of her computer terminal she suddenly remembered Frank Brannon's remark regarding the possibility of teaching computer operating techniques. Remark? she wondered. It almost seemed like a well thought out statement. In fact, many of the conversations at the Brannons' home had come across as contrived, preplanned. Now that she looked back on it, there had been some very unusual topics for a backyard barbecue.

Of course, the Brannons were not run-of-the-mill type people, but still . . . They had discussed the fine state of motherhood, the joys of being a Cub Scout leader, the need for greater communication in the family unit. Then Rachel had paraded her cherubs in the gate for a hug and a kiss. Strange. Had Chelsey missed a message that had been directed at her? Or was she reading something into a simple family gathering?

No, now wait a minute. Kathleen had said Mike needed more notice when Mitch wanted to get together. That meant Mitch must have set up the dinner after he had left Chelsey's house when she'd blabbed her head off and said she loved him. Oh, Lord, that was it! He'd panicked and run home to Mommy and Daddy and enlisted their help in bailing him out of a sticky situation.

Hence, the nice sermonette from Frank Brannon on

the exciting new job she could have teaching computer operations. Then they had tossed in the hearth and home stuff and the two little girls with the hope that the career angle now appeared far more appealing. What a rotten thing to do. Smooth and clever, but rotten.

So why, to cap off the evening, had Mitch made love to her? Unless he'd played out his hand, taken care of all the details, and knew he was about to call it quits. So what the heck? Why not take what was being offered before he hit the road? Oh, dear heaven, no! Mitch wasn't that cold and heartless. But he had promised nothing, made no declarations of undying love, or a commitment to their future. No, dammit, she wasn't going to think about it anymore. She was *not* going to be sad today. Not today.

Chelsey arrived home at six, took a quick shower before changing into jeans and a gauzy blouse, and ate a dinner of a hamburger and French fries. As she reached in the cupboard for a new bottle of catsup, her hand brushed the can of artichoke hearts. She stuffed it in the back out of sight.

If she didn't stop analyzing everything Mitch did, she was going to ruin whatever time they had left, she thought fiercely. She was mentally picking apart his actions and statements, looking for some clue as to his intentions. Why not wait and be surprised? She laughed, the sound hollow and bitter to her own ears. Lord, what was happening to her? She was acting so bitchy it was incredible. Did lovemaking turn her into a shrew?

"Now *that* was silly," she said to Zork. "I am simply a woman in love with a man who does not have the good sense to fall in love with me. Which, my dear Zork, is very depressing. Want a haircut, Zork? No, huh? Rats."

How weird, Chelsey thought as Mitch kissed her when he arrived, how the mere sight of the man could make her forget all her problems.

"Hello, Chelsey mine," he said, close to her lips.

"Hi." She smiled. "Good day?"

"Average."

"Did you take the Ferrari into the shop?"

"I didn't—"

"Have time. I don't understand, Mitch. You bought that car for your birthday. Don't you want to have it fixed so you can enjoy it? I even have the money now to pay for the windshield."

"Yeah, sure, I want it and I'll get to it real soon. What do you think you'll do with the rest of the money?" he asked, sinking onto the sofa.

"Like I said, pay for your broken windshield."

"Besides that."

"I don't know. Save it for an emergency, I guess."

"No!" he said sharply. "Don't do that!"

"Why not?" she asked, startled by his outburst.

"There has to be something you want. A dream, fantasy, whatever. Like a trip."

"Trip?" she repeated, an icy misery washing over her. "As in, leave town?"

"Haven't you ever had a desire to travel?"

"No, Mitch," she said, willing herself not to cry, "I have not. There's no place I want to go."

"Okay." He shrugged. "It was just a suggestion. Strike traveling from the list."

"What list? The same one that has furniture, new career, and artichoke hearts on it?"

"Oh, great," he said, raking his hand through his hair. "Here we go with the artichoke hearts again. Why do you keep doing that?"

"Me? Why do you insist on me making changes in my life? You're covering everything from my crummy sofa to my job and a bunch of stuff in between. Just what is it you're trying to tell me here?"

"Only what I said before. It's your turn to—to make some choices for yourself. There are options open to you that weren't there before because of your responsibility for Richard. I'm simply pointing out a few facts, that's all."

"Why?"

"Why?"

"You heard me, Mitch."

"I'm just trying to be helpful," he said, smiling at her engagingly.

"Oh, ha!"

"Come on, let's go see Annie. You're getting all uptight over nothing."

"I wouldn't call trying to shuffle me out of town nothing."

"I did no such thing! I thought you might like to have a vacation you'd always wanted. Forget I mentioned it, for Pete's sake. Besides, if you decide to teach you'll probably need some more college credits."

"Oh, now we're going to do that one!"

"Chelsey, stop it! I refuse to get in an argument about this. Hey." He grinned. "I make better love than war."

"Says who?"

"You! Annie awaits," he said, circling her shoulders with his arm.

Chelsey stared moodily out the side window of the truck as Mitch drove to the hospital. Dammit, she thought, why did Mitch always have an answer to everything? She'd ended up sounding ridiculous again. Had she overreacted to what was only idle chitchat?

But he seemed to be pushing her to spend every penny of the loan, go after some elusive dream she supposedly had. Didn't he realize that all she wanted was him and his returned love? Was a trip to wherever his idea of an instant cure for a broken heart? Why was Mitch beating around the bush like that? Or was she reading it all wrong? It was definitely driving her crazy!

"Slide over here, Chelsey," Mitch said. "You're too far away."

She settled against his strong shoulder and tried desperately to push the distressing thoughts from her mind. He was dismissing the earlier tension between them as if it had never occurred and so would she. She was boxing at shadows anyway, trying to understand a dilemma that might very well be a figment of her imagination. Life was complicated enough without inventing things to stew about.

Annie was holding court when they arrived at the hospital. The tiny woman had captured the hearts of the doctors and nurses and her room was a nonstop flow of people. Annie proudly introduced Chelsey and her Golden Boy, then a young intern showed up with a pizza and bottles of soda. A good time was had by all.

Chelsey was smiling when she left the hospital, her buoyant mood restored, and when Mitch suggested they go directly back to her house a tingle of anticipation swept through her. There was no mistaking the gleam in Mitch Brannon's blue eyes and Chelsey knew they would not be watching the fuzzy television.

Mitch would carry her away once again to that euphoric world and she would go willingly. She would be held safely within his strong embrace and there would be only the two of them. Nothing else beyond the sphere of their ecstasy would exist.

And so it was. In the glow of the silvery moonlight, Mitch kissed and caressed Chelsey until she was moaning with pleasure, calling to him to consume her with the essence of his being. He chanted her name over and over as they soared beyond reality, coming at last to a crescendo in perfect unison and splendor. Chelsey's love for Mitch seemed to reach to the deepest recesses of her soul, and she contentedly lay close to his side and gave way to the oblivion of sleep.

When Chelsey shut off the alarm the next morning, Mitch was gone. A note from him on the kitchen table said she should have a nice day and not work too hard. She frowned as she leaned against the counter and drank her coffee. She hated waking up to an empty bed, her lover having snuck out in the night like some kind of thief.

She, Chelsey Star, was having an affair! She, the original Victorian maiden, advocate of motherhood and apple pie, was involved in a modern-day, liberated tryst. How terrible! Magnificent during the throes of passion, but in the glaring light of day? Definitely hard on the conscience. But it was this or nothing. Mitch wasn't exactly sweeping her into his arms and carrying her over the threshold as his bride.

"But I love him, the bum," she said to Zork.

In the middle of the afternoon, Chelsey was called into her supervisor's office for the periodical review of her work performance. The man raved on and on about her excellent caliber of production, her outstanding dedication and attitude, and announced she would be receiving a raise in pay, effective immediately.

"How about that?" Chelsey said, beaming, when she informed Tony of the news.

"You deserve it, kid," he said. "You're the best. Well, second only after me."

"Of course." She smiled.

"So are you going to celebrate or something?"

"I guess so."

"Anything wrong, Chels?"

"No, Tony, I'm fine. How did it go with your nurse?"

"Not so good. Annie's a doll, but she's full of beans."

Chelsey shook her head ruefully as she walked home from the bus stop. A short time ago the extra money from the raise would have been the answer to her prayers, the means to make up the difference in what Richard was lacking from losing his job. But now she didn't really need it. She didn't even know what to spend the rest of Mitch's loan on and he seemed determined that every penny should have a definite purpose. Life certainly took some strange turns at times.

Chelsey had just changed into shorts and a top when Polly's voice came booming through the front door.

"Chelsey, are you home?" she yelled.

Mitch was right, Chelsey thought with a smile. Polly should knock like the rest of the world. "Come in!" she called.

"Hi," Polly said. "How's life?"

"I got a raise today."

"Hey, terrific. You ought to celebrate. Oh, I saw marvelous Mitch today. I was jumping up and down and waving but he didn't see me."

"What was he up to?"

"He came out of an attorney's office across the parking lot from the lawyer I work for."

"Brannon Development has a lot of legal business, I suppose," Chelsey said, scratching Zork's ears.

"I'm sure they do. I had to laugh, Chelsey. As if he isn't beautiful enough, he had on a royal blue shirt the exact shade of his Ferrari. The women must have been swooning in his path. He's so good-looking I can't—"

"What did you say?" Chelsey whispered.

"It's no news flash. You obviously know how handsome—"

"About the car. What was he driving?"

"A new Ferrari. Well, I'm off to water Annie's plants. See ya."

"Yeah, 'bye," Chelsey said absently. Mitch had lied! He kept claiming he didn't have time to get the windshield on the Ferrari fixed. He continually dismissed it as unimportant and something he'd get to when he could. Unless . . . Maybe he just hadn't mentioned he had taken it into the shop and would come roaring up in the sleek automobile tonight. Yes, of course, that was it! They'd go for a ride. Maybe he'd even let her drive it. Fat chance.

"Plants," Chelsey said. "I keep forgetting the roof isn't going to water them anymore!"

Her chore completed, Chelsey ate dinner. Since there was no sign of Mitch, she then went for a bike ride with Zork loping beside her, his candy apple red sunglasses securely in place. As she made her way back to the house her heart sank. Mitch's truck was parked in the driveway.

"Oh, Lord," she whispered, "the truck. Not the Ferrari, the damn truck."

"Hi, flash," Mitch greeted her as Chelsey jumped off the bike.

"Hello. I see you still haven't gotten the Ferrari fixed. Or have you?"

"No time, my sweet. Guess what I have? Fresh raspberries and a carton of cream. Let's go inside and pig out."

"I'll put my bike in the back," Chelsey said quietly. "Go on in the house."

Mitch was in the kitchen serving up the treat when she came in the back door. Dressed in faded jeans and a tan knit shirt he was magnificent, and Chelsey stood perfectly still drinking in the sight of him. He was carrying on an animated conversation with Zork and the Great Dane was wagging his tail happily in response.

"Mitch?" Chelsey said.

"Yeah, babe? Come have some of this. Look at the size of these berries!"

"Mitch, why did you lie to me about the Ferrari?"

"What?" He spun around to look at her.

"Why, Mitch?" she said, a catch in her voice as she fought the tears prickling at the back of her eyes.

"How did—I mean . . ."

"Polly saw you driving it today. She was all impressed because your shirt matched the car."

"Oh, man," he said, pushing his hand through his hair.

"How long has it been repaired?"

"Chelsey, I—"

"How long?" she said, her voice rising.

"Since a couple days after you did your Reggie Jackson bit, but—"

"You've had it all this time? Why did you lie to me?"

"Because I never had any intention of you paying for it!"

"What?"

"I knew I couldn't take your money from the minute I brought you home that day!"

"Because you felt sorry for me?" she yelled. "Has that what it has all been, Mitch? I was your do-gooder project for the year? Hey, I did pretty well here. I got new furniture, my roof repaired, tons of money, fatherly advice regarding my career from Frank Brannon and, best of all, I was relieved of my socially unacceptable virginity. I tell you, Mitch, when you take on a charity case you really do it up right."

"Dammit, don't you dare say such a thing. You can't possibly believe—"

"Can't I? What else am I supposed to think? I sure screwed it up when I fell in love with you, didn't I? But don't worry, I've decided to take your advice and go on a trip. A long one away from here, away from you! You can call off the Brannon troops. I'll disappear quietly."

"Chelsey, no! You don't understand!"

"Get out of my house," she said, her hands clenched at her sides. "Don't ever come back here. Not ever. I'll mail your loan payments and every one will be right on time."

"Chelsey, please, listen to me!" he said, starting toward her.

"Don't come near me! Don't touch me! Don't even smile. Just leave me alone! Go, Mitch! Now!"

"Chelsey, for God's sake, you've got it all wrong! I—Oh, all right, I'll go. I can't talk to you when you're like this. I'll give you time to calm down and then I'll be back. I *will* be back, Chelsey!"

She stood statue still, hardly breathing as Mitch turned and stalked from the room. The loud slamming of the front door made her jump, then she gave way to the sobs that racked her body. Stumbling into the living room she flung herself onto the sofa and cried until there was nothing left but a chilling emptiness within her. Darkness had long since settled over the small house, but she made no attempt to turn on the lights. She just stared up at a ceiling she couldn't see.

What a fool she had been, she thought miserably. She had ignored Tony's and Polly's warnings and had listened only to her heart. She had fallen in love with a man she was convinced was her Prince Charming, thrown caution to the wind, and given herself totally— heart, mind, body, and soul—into his care.

To Mitch she had been nothing more than a pitiful creature who struggled to make ends meet and lived in a house with a leaky roof. She had been his project, his raison d'être to compensate for his wealth and worry-free existence. He no doubt patted himself on the back for his magnanimous gestures on her behalf.

But how was she going to survive without him? He had become the focal point of her existence. Her smiles were produced by his, her laughter genuine only when mingled with his. She lived for the times he was with her and missed him instantly when he was gone. He had awakened her femininity from its lifelong slumber and nurtured it to bloom. And now it was over. Mitch was gone and she was left only with memories and the ache in her heart.

The remainder of the week was a blur to Chelsey. She hardly slept or ate, went through her day at work as automated and mechanical as the computers that glared at her with their maddening green screens. Tony was engrossed in a rush project and she was relieved that he had no time to chat. When Polly pressed her for an explanation for the dark circles under her eyes, Chelsey wept through her tale of woe as Polly shook her head and frowned.

From Mitch, Chelsey heard nothing.

On Saturday morning she realized she was dreading the weekend and its endless stretch of empty hours. She was unable to muster any enthusiasm for working in the garden, or baking bread, or cleaning her house. She wanted to see Mitch Brannon and nothing else held any appeal.

"Chelsey! Chelsey! Chelsey!" Polly suddenly yelled as she came barreling in the front door.

"Good grief!" Chelsey said. "You scared me to death. Whatever is the matter with you?"

"I can't believe it! Outside there's a—I just can't believe it! I have never in my life—I can't believe it!"

"Polly, what is it?"

"Coming down the street! Chelsey, get out there." Polly grabbed her by the arm and hauled her through the front door.

"Polly, I'm really not in the mood to— My God," Chelsey gasped.

With a slow, steady, clip-clop cadence, walking right down the middle of the street, was the biggest, whitest horse Chelsey had ever seen. And sitting high in the saddle, complete with a flowing red velvet robe and a many-pointed crown, was Mitchell Michael Brannon!

"Mitch?" Chelsey whispered, her eyes widening as the horse and rider approached, followed by the people in the neighborhood who came tumbling out of their houses.

He stopped the horse right in the middle of her lawn, dismounted, and bowed deeply in front of her. He was wearing a white tuxedo beneath the robe and Chelsey simply gawked at him, her mouth open.

"Chelsey Star," Mitch boomed for all to hear, "I am your Prince Charming!"

"My who?" she asked, blinking once slowly.

"You see before you," he went on, "your very own, one to a customer, to keep for a lifetime, Prince Charming!"

"I'm going to cry," Polly said. "Oh, this is so romantic."

"Chelsey Star, will you marry me? Will you ride with me to my castle and be my princess?"

"I—um—what?" Chelsey said.

"Splendid!" Mitch said. He scooped her up and planted her firmly on the saddle, then swung up behind her.

"Mitch, no!" she said, finally coming out of her fog. "This is crazy! Put me down."

"Farewell, kind friends," Mitch said, and a cheer went up from the gathering.

"Mitch, this is kidnapping," Chelsey said as they set off down the street.

"Don't be silly." He grinned. "All princes do this. It's in the handbook."

"Mitch, I'm warning you . . ."

"Hush thy mouth, princess mine. We shall speak beneath yon tree."

"Oh, for Pete's sake," Chelsey said, rolling her eyes.

Mitch swung out of the saddle and lifted Chelsey to the ground. He tied the reins of the enormous horse to a limb of the tree, then removed his crown and cape and pulled Chelsey down onto the grass with him.

"Snazzy suit, huh?" he said, looking at his tuxedo. "Maybe I'll wear this when we get married."

"We are not getting—"

Chelsey's sputtering was silenced by a long, heavenly kiss that left her breathless.

"Thanks," Mitch said. "I needed that. I've missed you so much, Chelsey."

"I . . ."

"There's something you should know. I love you, Chelsey Star. I love you with every breath in my body. I think I fell in love with you the day you thought you were Reggie Jackson. When you stood there peering up at me from under the bill of that baseball cap, chomping on your gum, with your goofy sunglasses-wearing dog standing next to you, I knew my life was about to undergo a major change."

"You love me?" she asked hesitantly.

"Oh, yes, I do."

"Then why did you insist I fix up my house and buy me artichoke hearts and—"

"Could you just pass by the artichoke hearts? They're really getting on my nerves."

"Mitch, you urged me to go after a new career. You even told me to leave town! That doesn't sound like a man in love to me."

"You've got to understand where I was coming from. You'd been struggling for so long because you were helping Richard and the end was at last in sight. In a few months you'd be able to do anything you wanted to. Lord, Chelsey, I came so close to telling you so many times that I loved you, wanted to marry you, but I was scared to death."

"But why?"

"Because, babe, you'd never had your turn. I was so afraid you'd suddenly find yourself married and realize you'd never gone after your own dreams before you settled down. I kept dangling ideas under your nose, praying I wouldn't see your face light up and off you'd go. I didn't want to rob you of your fantasies by loving you, Chelsey, so I never told you how I felt."

"But you made love to me, Mitch."

"I wasn't going to until I knew you were sure a life with me was what you truly wanted. That's why I kept changing my tactics on the subject, trying to keep you off balance. But when you said you were in love with me, my chances to win you forever were looking better all the time. I made love to you to show you how beautiful that part of our life would be together. Maybe it wasn't totally fair, but I was getting desperate. I dropped you in the middle of my parents' backyard because they're so very happy as husband and wife and—"

"Had Rachel parade her lovely children in front of me," Chelsey said, starting to smile.

"Yeah, she was in on it too. My whole family was. They knew I loved you, but was trying to give you enough space to really get in touch with yourself. I didn't want to smother you with my love, Chelsey. Freedom was within your grasp and I couldn't rob you of it."

"Oh, Mitch, I love you so much. There's nothing out there that could possibly compare to being your wife and the mother of your babies. That's my dream, Mitch. You're all I want or need."

"Oh, Chelsey, we're going to have a wonderful life together."

"I should be furious with you about the Ferrari."

"That's *our* car. A man doesn't send a bill to his own wife. That is, I mean . . . Chelsey, will you marry me? Will you be my partner for the remainder of our days?"

"Yes! Oh, yes, Mitch."

"Oh, man, I am the luckiest guy in the world! You know, maybe Polly will move into your house to get away from her nympho roommate and then Annie would be looked after and— See what you've done to me? I'm all caught up in the beautiful world you live in."

"And as an extra bonus you get Zork and Myrtle!"

"Sounds good to me, Chelsey mine. Oh, on our fiftieth wedding anniversary we'll have an in-depth discussion on the subject of artichoke hearts and you can explain what that has been all about. For now, let's get out of here. People are staring at us for some reason. You'd think they'd never seen a man in a white tuxedo sitting on the grass next to a gorgeous lady and a very large horse."

"What they don't realize is that what they are seeing is an honest-to-goodness Prince Charming," Chelsey said, happy tears clinging to her lashes. "And he's all mine, the one I've been waiting for."

Mitch gathered her into his arms and kissed her deeply as Chelsey's heart soared with love. At midnight every clock in the city would chime the hour and still her dream would not be over. She would be with Mitchell Michael Brannon for the remainder of her days.

"Let's go home, Cinderella," he said softly.

"Forever, Prince Charming," she said. "Forever."

THE EDITOR'S CORNER

With this month's books we begin our *third* year of publishing LOVESWEPT. And are we excited about it! It feels as though we've only just begun, and I hope our enthusiasm for the love stories coming up next year is matched by your enjoyment of them.

Publishers work far in advance of the dates books reach the public. Did you know that producing a LOVESWEPT romance takes the same amount of time as a baby? That's right, nine full months! Even as you are reading this we are sending to our Production Department the LOVESWEPTS for January *1986*. So, with great certainty, I can assure you that our third year will continue the tradition of emotional and exceptional romances you've come to expect from LOVESWEPT. I envy you. I wish I had all the great forthcoming LOVESWEPTS to enjoy for the first time. But, then, you should just see what delicious stuff is on my desk right now for 1986! Back to next month, now, and the "four pleasures" in store for you.

Marvelous Barbara Boswell is back with **DARLING OBSTACLES**, LOVESWEPT #95. The title refers to the seven children the heroine and hero (both widowed) have between them. Never have there been seven more rowdy or adorable snags to romance. Maggie May is poor and very proud and the babysitter of surgeon Greg Wilder's three youngest children. Wrapped in their own concerns, neither parent has taken a good long look at the other until one chilly night when Greg comes to pick up his kids . . . and then the magic starts! **DARLING OBSTACLES** is genuinely heartwarming and deeply thrilling. Nine cheers for Barbara Boswell!

(continued)

Passionate and intense, **ENCHANTMENT,** LOVE-SWEPT #96, by Kimberli Wagner is a riveting love story full of sensual tension between two dramatic characters. Alex Kouris and Rhea Morgan are both artists and both mesmerized by one another when they meet. They know immediately that they are kindred souls . . . yet each has a problem to come to terms with before they can realize their destiny together. You won't want to miss Kim's breathtaking romance, which is truly full of **ENCHANTMENT.**

All of us on the LOVESWEPT staff are as fond of Adrienne Staff and Sally Goldenbaum as we are admiring of their skill at creating a unique love story. They make their debut with us in **WHAT'S A NICE GIRL . . . ?,** LOVESWEPT #97. This is the wonderfully humorous and truly touching romance of Susan Rosten and Logan Reed—two people who were meant to find one another across an ocean of differences. Susan comes from a boisterous, warm, close-knit Jewish family; Logan is a rather staid member of the "country club set." Susan owns and operates a local tavern; Logan is a distinguished physician. The resolution of the conflicts between them is often merry, sometimes serious, and always emotionally moving. We believe that after reading **WHAT'S A NICE GIRL . . . ?** you'll be as enthusiastic fans of Adrienne's and Sally's as we are.

And rounding out the month is a superb romance from that superb writer Fayrene Preston. **MISSISSIPPI BLUES,** LOVESWEPT #98, is as witty, as sensually evocative, as emotionally involving as a love story can be! You'll be delighted from the first moments of the provocative (and most unusual) opening of this story until the very last. Fayrene's brash Yankee hero, Kane Benedict, falls for winsome heroine, Suzanna de Francesca, a tenderhearted, passionate woman who has three extraordinary people for whom she's responsible. Suzanna's need to protect her home and its residents clashes violently with Kane's interest in her community. Yet the sultry attraction between them won't—*can't*—be stopped. The charm of Magnolia Trails and the love of Kane and Suzanna will linger with you long after you've finished **MISSISSIPPI BLUES**.

Enjoy!
Sincerely,

Carolyn Nichols

Carolyn Nichols
  Editor
LOVESWEPT
Bantam Books, Inc.
666 Fifth Avenue
New York, NY 10103

Dear Reader:

Meet Belinda Stuart—talented, beautiful, and about to embark on a new life as a successful painter. The only dark place in her heart is occupied by Jack, the tormented husband from whom she has had to separate. Suddenly, just as she's getting her act together, the past comes back to tear her apart.

Back in their carefree days at Harvard, Belinda and her best friend Sally met the men they would marry. Both Jack Stuart and Harry Granger were part of a group who jokingly referred to themselves as "the Ruffians," an irresistibly boisterous club whose loyalty to each other lasted long after their college years. Belinda, captivated by Jack's winning good looks and his talent as a writer, chose him over Harry, but it was Harry who went on to literary fame.

When Harry's hit musical opens in New York, all the Ruffians are there to cheer their friend's success. Two days later tragedy has struck—one of the Ruffians has been murdered, shot point blank in the doorway of Sally and Harry's house. And Belinda is forced to face the fact that the murder is related to her—although she has no idea why.

One by one, every man Belinda has known turns up in the present—Peter Venables, who once loved Belinda and can't believe she doesn't feel the same way for him; Mike Pierce, the perfect gentleman who treats Belinda like a beautiful younger sister; even Harry, Belinda and Jack's most trusted friend—each man with a conflicting story to tell. One is a cold-blooded killer; all prefer to blame Jack than face the horrible truth.

When Belinda and Jack were married, Sally was determined to give them the perfect wedding present, an antique wheel of fortune that would foretell their happy lives together. But now Belinda must return, alone, to the past. She has to uncover the dark secret that has already claimed the life of one person—and may soon claim her own.

Let Dana Clarins thrill you with Belinda's spellbinding story, the unforgettable tale of what happens when a beautiful woman wakes to find herself, alone and frightened, in the middle of her own worst nightmare.

Dana Clarins is a bestselling writer whose books have sold millions of copies under another name. GUILTY PARTIES is the best yet. I'm betting you won't be able to put it down!

Warm regards,

Nessa Rapoport

Nessa Rapoport
Senior Editor

S ALLY CAME OFF THE ELEVATOR carrying in her arms, like a gigantic infant, a cascade of yellow roses wrapped in tissue, tied loosely with a thick yellow ribbon, a floppy bow. She marched on into the kitchen and began searching for vases.

"What in the world—" I said.

"You've got paint all over your face, dear. Two vases aren't going to be enough." She was wearing a pale blue linen dress, sleeveless, with white piping. She was too pale herself for the outfit but with the jet-black hair and the sharp angles of her face she looked great.

I found her a third vase. "What is this?"

"For you. They were propped on that pathetic little wooden chair down in the lobby. Just sitting there. I asked a man carrying a box bigger than East Rutherford into the warehouse if he'd seen them delivered. He told me he couldn't see where he was going, let alone check out deliverymen. Here's a card."

I tore open the envelope.

Apologies are in order. I'll make them in person.

The fan on the counter passed its waves across my face like the flutter of invisible wings, and I felt a shiver ripple along my spine. Sally was watching me, hands on hips, feet apart, waiting impatiently. "So what does it say?"

I handed it to her and she cocked her head inquisitively. The light at the windows was reflecting the deep purple of the afternoon sky. The first raindrops were tapping on the skylight. I couldn't tell her about Venables. I'd told him I wouldn't and he was their houseguest on top of that and the show was opening and who needed any more problems?

And Sal and I didn't tell each other everything, anyway. Not anymore.

"May I ask what that is supposed to mean?"

I made a face. "It's nothing. A guy . . . a guy I barely know made a mistake the other night . . ." I shrugged.

"Ah, the adventures of the newly single!" She picked up two of the vases and smiled at me quizzically. "Well,

I won't pry. But let it be recorded that I am utterly fascinated."

"It's not very fascinating. Let that be recorded."

I followed her into the work area. The thunder's first crack went off like a cannon and I flinched. Like a child frightened by loud noises and the gathering darkness.

"I'm betting on Jack. Or—hmmm—could it be Mike?"

"What? What are you talking about?"

"Belinda, are you all right?"

"Yes, of course, I'm fine."

"The flowers. I was talking about the flowers—I'll bet they're from Jack, who misbehaved and is sorry . . . or from Mike. I mean, you have been seeing Mike—"

"Please, Sal. Mike is an old friend. You know that—we've had dinner a couple of times and Mike is the spitting image of Bertie Wooster and he's a dear. But he never, never would make a mistake about me. Okay? I rest my case."

Sally was leaning against the wheel-of-fortune, staring out into the rain, nodding. I mopped sweat from my face and dropped the towel on the table.

"All right, all right. It's your secret." She pressed a forefinger to her lips, looking at me from the corners of her eyes. . . .

The afternoon wore on. The loft darkened. Lightning continued to crackle over the city like electrical stems, jagged, plunging down into the heart of Manhattan. The rain came down like dishwater emptying out of a sink. Sally had another drink and sucked on the bright green wedge of lime. The yellow roses glowed as if they were lit from within. I listened to Sally talk about men, the show, Harry and Jack. . . .

One moment she was laughing and then the thunder hammered at the skylight again and her face began to come apart and redefine itself as if she were about to burst into tears.

"Are you all right, Sal?" I went to her, wanting to help. She turned quickly away, back to the wheel-of-fortune.

"Let's see what the gods hold for tonight, a hit or a miss." She sniffled, spun the wheel, planted her feet apart as if challenging the future. It finally clicked to a halt.

Sal read it slowly. "'You will have everything you have hoped for.'"

She looked at me, trying to smile.

"Oh," she said, "everything is such a mess, honey." She began to cry with her head on my shoulder. I put my arm around her, felt the shuddering as Sally clung to me. I cooed to her. Everything would be all right. But as I stroked her shiny black hair, the paintings in the shadows caught my eye and I wasn't sure.

*   *   *

AT SIX O'CLOCK THE CROWD clogged the street in front of the theater, the lucky ones squeezed beneath the marquee with its *Scoundrels All!* logo in Harvard crimson. Everyone was dressed up and soaked through with perspiration and sprays of rain. Everyone seemed to be shouting to be heard, faces were red, laughter too loud. Bright, artificial smiles looked like the direct result of root-canal work. Hope was everywhere. The sight made me wonder if my own opening would be so frantic, so harried, so riddled with fear and tension.

I held onto Mike's arm, smiled faintly at familiar faces, and nodded at snatches of conversation I couldn't quite make out. The whole scene was a kind of orgy of self-consciousness, people with a good deal to lose but trying not to show it, pretending that nothing hung in the balance. Another opening, another show.

Harry's head was visible above the crowd, inclined to the comments of two men I recognized by sight, one a legendary womanizer and show-business angel, the other a famous agent who knew everyone and never missed anything. At a party once years before I'd seen him take a package of chewing gum from the beringed hand of a very young woman with turquoise and purple hair and Jack had whispered to me: "See that? That's how they do it. Cocaine wrapped in five little sticks, like gum." He'd been terribly amused when at first I couldn't believe it.

A large, bulky man in a very crumpled linen jacket with a floppy silk handkerchief dribbling from the pocket looked benignly out across the crowd from Harry's side. He alone seemed serene and somewhat amused by the proceedings, as if his cumbersome size kept him from becoming too frantic. I'd seen him before, I was sure of it, but where? I was watching him without really being aware of it when he caught my eye, seemed to be staring at me, expressionless. Then, as if he'd made a connection that was just eluding me, he slowly grinned and I looked away. Should I have known him? He wasn't the type you'd forget.

Mike was waving at people, chattering away. The show's director stood more or less alone, a tiny bearded man, looking like a child's toy wound right to the breaking point. He glanced at his watch, then disappeared through the stage door. Slowly the crowd began to push through the doors, through the lobby, down the red-carpeted aisles toward their seats. The black uniformed ushers whisked up and down, checking tickets, handing out programs.

My stomach was knotted, my throat dry, and I wondered how Sally was holding up. I couldn't see her in the crowd. Mike Nichols was a few rows ahead of us, standing, still wearing a rain-spotted, belted trench coat, his face amazingly boyish beneath the blondish hair. There was Tony LoBianco, dark and handsome, radiating energy and intensity, as if he were about to spring at someone or something. Doc Simon, shy and tall and scholarly, was talking to a man who looked like a banker, which figured, since the playwright had finally, officially, made all the money in the known universe.

Scanning the faces, I knew I was actually looking for the two I hoped most weren't there. Jack. And Peter Venables. The thought of both men was pushing my stomach off center. Praying I wouldn't turn and come face to face with them, praying for the easy way out. I kept thinking of Jack slamming the phone down and cutting Sally off . . . and Peter's beautiful yellow roses and the note that filled me with dread. *Apologies are in order. I'll make them in person.*

Finally, thank God, the houselights dimmed and I hadn't seen either of them.

Within seconds I felt as if the curtain had gone up on a kind of personal psychodrama, as if I'd stumbled straight off the edge of the real world and was free-falling through time.

*   *   *

FOR SOME REASON THAT SUMMER nobody had quite bothered to prepare me for the show I saw. Maybe it was because I had been so wrapped up in my own work, maybe because I hadn't been listening when they tried. Whatever the reason, I wasn't in the least prepared once the actors and actresses had taken the stage, and it was hard to shake free of the disorientation.

With music and dancing and a witty book, *Scoundrels All!* was *our* story, the story of the Ruffians and Sally and me, and it came at me in a series of waves, reviving memories I'd never known were buried in my subconscious, memories of people and events I hadn't been aware of at the time. It was like seeing one of Alex Katz's paintings in a Fifty-seventh Street gallery, a scene of his sharp-featured people at a cocktail party, pretty women with flat, predatory looks, well-dressed men with cuffs showing just the right amount as they climbed one social or business ladder after another . . . like seeing the paintings and slowly realizing that you were there, you'd been one of the people at the party. It was both unnerving and seductive and I felt myself almost guiltily being excited by what I saw, as if it were my own private secret.

I'd been so wrapped up in my own concerns in those days that I'd hardly noticed the world around me. Classes, clothes, time spent with Sally, driving her little red convertible along narrow leaf-blown roads, working in the studio at all hours, painting and losing track of time, then meeting Harry Granger . . . and later Jack Stuart.

Now, astonished, I watched all our lives cavorting across the stage, laughter rippling and applause exploding from the audience. Reality had been softened and given pastel hues at it was filtered through the lens of nostalgia. Like a faint recollection that had almost slipped through the cracks of memory, my past was coming back to life, and we were all up there on the stage. Whatever names they were called, they were us. Jack, the athlete with the handsome face, tossing a football in the air, singing a song about the big game Saturday with Yale . . . Mike wearing white duck slacks and a straw boater at a jaunty angle, dancing an engaging soft-shoe . . . Harry politicking his friends about his idea for a club, an oath of loyalty, and a commitment for a lifetime, all so innocent and idealistic . . . and there were the girls, a blond and a brunette arriving on the stage in a snazzy red convertible.

I was having some difficulty keeping the lines between fact and fiction from blurring. Which was the real Belinda? The one on stage or the nearly middle-aged one watching? Did I really say that? Is that the way I behaved, the way I appeared to others—the self-centered ultra-Wasp who seemed to pluck for herself first one man and then the other?

The love stories wound sinuously, sometimes comically, through the saga of the founding of the club and the conflicts among the members and the crisis of the football game . . . Harry falling in love with the blond, then losing her to Jack, then Harry taking sudden notice of the brunette.

But it was all in a kind of fairyland where the hurts never lasted and everybody finally loved everyone else and everything was all right. . . . Jack was singing alone in a spotlight, wearing a corny letter sweater with the flickering illusion of a pep-rally bonfire through a scrim behind him. Not much like Harvard, really, it might have been an artifact like the Thurber and Nugent play, *The Male Animal*, it all seemed so quaint and long ago. Jack was singing about the blond girl he'd fallen for and how he was going to have to take her away from his best pal Harry and would it wreck their friendship and how could one Scoundrel do such a thing to another?

And, like a sentimental fool, I thanked God for the darkness of the theater. My cheek was wet with tears.

A Stirring Novel of Destinies
Bound by Unquenchable Passion

SUNSET
EMBRACE

by Sandra Brown

Fate threw Lydia Russell and Ross Coleman, two untamed
outcasts, together on a Texas-bound wagon train. On that wild
road, they fought the breathtaking desire blazing between them,
while the shadows of their enemies grew longer. As the train
rolled west, danger drew ever closer, until a showdown with
their pursuers was inevitable. Before it was over, Lydia and
Ross would face death . . . the truth about each other . . . and
the astonishing strength of·their love.

Buy SUNSET EMBRACE, on sale January 15, 1985
wherever Bantam paperbacks are sold, or use the handy coupon below for ordering:

A stunning novel of romance and intrigue by

THE FOREVER DREAM

by Iris Johansen

Tania Orlinov is prima ballerina for a New York ballet company. Jared Ryker is a brilliant scientist whose genetics research has brought him to the brink of discovering how to extend human life for up to 500 years. A chance meeting brings them together—and now nothing can keep them apart.

THE FOREVER DREAM has all the passion, extraordinarily sensual lovemaking and romance that have become Iris Johansen's signature, plus the tension and suspense of a first-rate thriller. In her longest and most far-reaching novel to date, Iris Johansen taps all our fantasies of romantic love and explores the fascinating implications of practical immortality.

Don't miss THE FOREVER DREAM, available wherever Bantam Books are sold, or use this handy coupon for ordering:

Murdock's motives for pursuing her? Guilt? Pity? Casey had to choose. She could live with doubt and fear . . . or learn a lesson in love.

#7 A TRYST WITH MR. LINCOLN?

By Billie Green
When Jiggs O'Malley awakened in a strange hotel room, all she saw were the laughing eyes of stranger Matt Brady . . . all she heard were his teasing taunts about their "night together" . . . and all she remembered was nothing! They evaded the passions that intoxicated them until . . . there was nowhere to flee but into each other's arms.

#8 TEMPTATION'S STING

By Helen Conrad
Taylor Winfield likened Rachel Davidson to a Conus shell, contradictory and impenetrable. Rachel battled for independence, torn by her need for Taylor's embraces and her impassioned desire to be her own woman. Could they both succumb to the

temptation of the tropical paradise and still be true to their hearts?

#9 DECEMBER 32nd . . . AND ALWAYS

By Marie Michael
Blaise Hamilton made her feel like the most desirable woman on earth. Pat opened herself to emotions she'd thought buried with her late husband. Together they were unbeatable as they worked to build the jet of her late husband's dreams. Time seemed to be running out and yet—would ALWAYS be long enough?

#10 HARD DRIVIN' MAN

By Nancy Carlson
Sabrina sensed Jacy in hot pursuit, as she maneuvered her truck around the racetrack, and recalled his arms clasping her to him. Was he only using her feelings so he could take over her trucking company? Their passion knew no limits as they raced full speed toward love.

#11 BELOVED INTRUDER

By Noelle Berry McCue
Shannon Douglas hated

Michael Brady from the moment he brought the breezes of life into her shadowy existence. Yet a specter of the past remained to torment her and threaten their future. Could he subdue the demons that haunted her, and carry her to true happiness?

#12 HUNTER'S PAYNE
By Joan J. Domning
P. Lee Payne strode into Karen Hunter's office demanding to know why she was stalking him. She was determined to interview the mysterious photographer. She uncovered his concealed emotions, but could the secrets their hearts confided protect their love, or would harsh daylight shatter their fragile alliance?

#13 TIGER LADY
By Joan J. Domning
Who *was* this mysterious lover she'd never seen who courted her on the office computer, and nicknamed her Tiger Lady? And could he compete with Larry Hart, who came to repair the computer and stayed to short-cir-

cuit her emotions? How could she choose between poetry and passion—between soul and Hart?

#14 STORMY VOWS
By Iris Johansen
Independent Brenna Sloan wasn't strong enough to reach out for the love she needed, and Michael Donovan knew only how to take—until he met Brenna. Only after a misunderstanding nearly destroyed their happiness, did they surrender to their fiery passion.

#15 BRIEF DELIGHT
By Helen Mittermeyer
Darius Chadwick felt his chest tighten with desire as Cygnet Melton glided into his life. But a prelude was all they knew before Cyg fled in despair, certain she had shattered the dream they had made together. Their hearts had collided in an instant; now could they seize the joy of enduring love?

#16 A VERY RELUCTANT KNIGHT
By Billie Green
A tornado brought them together in a storm cel-

lar. But Maggie Sims and Mark Wilding were anything but perfectly matched. Maggie wanted to prove he was wrong about her. She knew they didn't belong together, but when he caressed her, she was swept up in a passion that promised a lifetime of love.

#17 TEMPEST AT SEA
By Iris Johansen
Jane Smith sneaked aboard playboy-director Jake Dominic's yacht on a dare. The muscled arms that captured her were inescapable—and suddenly Jane found herself agreeing to a month-long cruise of the Caribbean. Jane had never given much thought to love, but under Jake's tutelage she discovered its magic . . . and its torment.

#18 AUTUMN FLAMES
By Sara Orwig
Lily Dunbar had ventured too far into the wilderness of Reece Wakefield's vast Chilean ranch; now an oncoming storm thrust her into his arms . . . and he refused to let her go. Could he lure her, step by seductive step, away from the life she had forged for herself, to find her real home in his arms?

#19 PFARR LAKE AFFAIR
By Joan J. Domning
Leslie Pfarr hadn't been back at her father's resort for an hour before she was pitched into the lake by Eric Nordstrom! The brash teenager who'd made her childhood a constant torment had grown into a handsome man. But when he began persuading her to fall in love, Leslie wondered if she was courting disaster.

#20 HEART ON A STRING
By Carla Neggers
One look at heart surgeon Paul Houghton Welling told JoAnna Radcliff he belonged in the stuffy society world she'd escaped for a cottage in Pigeon Cove. She firmly believed she'd never fit into his life, but he set out to show her she was wrong. She was the puppet master, but he knew how to keep her heart on a string.

#21 THE SEDUCTION OF JASON
By Fayrene Preston
On vacation in Martinique, Morgan Saunders found Jason Falco. When a misunderstanding drove him away, she had to win him back. She played the seductress to tempt him to return; she sent him tropical flowers to tantalize him; she wrote her love in letters twenty feet high—on a billboard that echoed the words in her heart.

#22 BREAKFAST IN BED
By Sandra Brown
For all Sloan Fairchild knew, Hollywood had moved to San Francisco when mystery writer Carter Madison stepped into her bed-and-breakfast inn. In his arms the forbidden longing that throbbed between them erupted. Sloan had to choose—between her love for him and her loyalty to a friend . . .

#23 TAKING SAVANNAH
By Becky Combs
The Mercedes was headed straight for her! Cassie hurled a rock that smashed the antique car's taillight. The price driver Jake Kilrain exacted was a passionate kiss, and he set out to woo the Southern lady, Cassie, but discovered that his efforts to conquer the lady might end in his own surrender . . .

#24 THE RELUCTANT LARK
By Iris Johansen
Her haunting voice had earned Sheena Reardon fame as Ireland's mournful dove. Yet to Rand Challon the young singer was not just a lark but a woman whom he desired with all his heart. Rand knew he could teach her to spread her wings and fly free, but would her flight take her from him or into his arms forever?

 **LOVESWEPT**

Love Stories you'll never forget by authors you'll always remember

---

Prices and availability subject to change without notice.

Buy them at your local bookstore or use this handy coupon for ordering:

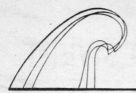 **LOVESWEPT**

Love Stories you'll never forget by authors you'll always remember

Prices and availability subject to change without notice.

Buy them at your local bookstore or use this handy coupon for ordering: